This Little Light

Finding Grace on the Road to Recovery

JAY DEPOY

WESTBOW
PRESS®
A DIVISION OF THOMAS NELSON
& ZONDERVAN

WestBow Press books may be ordered through booksellers or by contacting:

WestBow Press
A Division of Thomas Nelson & Zondervan
1663 Liberty Drive
Bloomington, IN 47403
www.westbowpress.com
1 (866) 928-1240

ISBN: 978-1-5127-6706-3 (sc)

Print information available on the last page.

WestBow Press rev. date: 12/15/2016

For Mariah Grace. Because we have known sad days, and happy days, and through them all – you have kept the light on for me. (Look out, Braodway!)

For Ambria Faith. Because one day I turned around and saw you following me up a hill, and I fell in love with you, my daughter.

For Ashlyn Hope. Because every night you insist that we sing four songs… "and some glad morning, we'll fly away!"

For Teresa Joy. Because you came into my life like a whirlwind of mercy, and restored my heart one piece at a time. Love has won.

This little light of mine, I'm gonna let it shine
This little light of mine, I'm gonna let it shine,
This little light of mine, I'm gonna let it shine,
Let it shine, let it shine, let it shine
Let it shine, let it shine, let it shine

Let it shine 'til Jesus comes
I'm gonna let it shine
Let it shine 'til Jesus comes
I'm gonna let it shine,
Let it shine 'til Jesus comes
I'm gonna let it shine

Let it shine, let it shine, let it shine

Foreword

Typically when I'm asked to write a forward to a book, I sit down with the manuscript for about an hour, flip through the highlights, and write an introduction.

Not so with Jay DePoy's book, *This Little Light.* I sat down with the manuscript Sunday after church and five hours later I was still transfixed. As I read the book, word for word, unable to skim, I cried, I prayed, and I went for long walks contemplating passages I'd just read.

This book communicates the depths of despair that most of us will experience at some point in our lives. It communicates the power of relationships, the pain of deception, and the horror each of us face when we meet our own sinful natures.

Jay encourages us to get back up and keep going. That has been a theme of mine for the last 10 years. I think of Judas and Peter both denying the Lord. Judas killed himself in despair and to this day we remember him as a traitor. But Peter kept going, so we don't see his betrayal of Christ as that significant because he had powerful ministry when he repented, got back up, and kept going.

In our modern context, we see a similar scenario played out in the lives of Richard Nixon and Bill Clinton. After Richard Nixon's scandal, he resigned, moved to California, and died. To this day, Watergate looms in our minds when we think of Nixon. Clinton went through a worse scandal, but kept going. Today that scandal not only fails to define his life, but as time passes and he keeps serving, the scandal shrinks from being his life story to being a chapter, then a page, and now probably a paragraph. Believe it or not, this story parallels the Christian experience.

As Jay so perfectly models in his book, if we can just keep going, the sun will eventually rise again.

The writing, the ideas, the character development, and the overall message are powerful. This is an excellent book. Enjoy.

- Rev. Ted Haggard

Senior Pastor, St. James Church in Colorado Springs, CO
Former President of the *National Association of Evangelicals*

The Beginning of the End

I stood trembling in the presence of Grace as Sierra emerged from the front door. Despite the cold December wind, she wasn't wearing a jacket or shoes. Her hair was longer since the last time I'd seen her, and she maintained the atomic beauty that held me captive all these years.

Somewhere between then and now, I must have become unrecognizable to her. Where shame had painted my conscience with self-inflicted scars, mercy covered the wounds. I was no longer afraid to look in her eyes, and in this moment I could not turn away.

Sierra stood like a silhouette on the front porch. She locked eyes with me as she planted her hands on her hips.

"Jordan," she said. "Where have you been?"

Chapter 1

The End of the Beginning

I remember the first time I felt the shattering suffocation of invisibility. When I was a sophomore in high school, an acquaintance nominated me for student council. I knew I had very little chance of actually winning, but a small piece of me was decimated by the fact that out of the several hundred students at South Charleston Senior High School, I had not tallied a single vote. Not one. Apparently the classmate who nominated me only did so as a joke, and when it came time to cast our ballots, he didn't even vote for me. But I didn't blame him, or anyone else, because I didn't vote for myself either.

For most of my life, I had been known only as the son of Tom Winter, who was often the subject of much conversation. My dad was not a closet drinker; he was a sit-on-the-front-porch drunk who was accustomed to cussing out pedestrians on the sidewalk or stumbling around the front yard in his underwear. On the night of my thirteenth birthday, my dad celebrated with his friends, Jack Daniels and Jim Beam, and loaded up behind the wheel of his Ford truck. The impending legacy would be a scar that would shame our family for the rest of my life. That evening, my dad swerved into the oncoming traffic lane and crashed into a minivan. Two children were killed, and my dad would spend the rest of his natural life in a South Carolina State Penitentiary. Yes, I am the

1

son of Tom Winter, and I dreamed of personal redemption every day of my life.

I was an only child, and it must have been hard for my mother to relate to me. A few years after my dad's incarceration, my mom went through a series of relationships and I was virtually left to raise myself. Even when she was in the same room, my mother always seemed absent.

My grades reflected the indifference in my heart, my self-esteem measured by the number of unexcused absences I had tallied by eleventh grade, at which point the Department of Child Services got involved. My caseworker intervened until the day I was sent to live with my aunt on the other side of town.

My mom's sister Tracy had no children of her own, so she lavished me with attention. Her desire to be "the cool aunt" allowed for me to get away with murder. She gave me my first drink, and never enforced a curfew. Aunt Tracy was once beautiful, and her hallway was a virtual shrine to years gone by. Her glory days of local beauty pageantry had long since passed by the time I moved in, but framed pictures told a thousand stories of tiaras and roses.

My mother would stop by occasionally, usually to borrow money from her sister or see what was in the refrigerator. I would sometimes find a note on the counter, saying she'd stopped by to see me. Even then, I felt a growing resentment toward her for the concrete distance between us.

By my senior year, I had become accustomed to front-porch drinking, repeating my father's mistakes, and fist-fighting with local cops. I hated my dad, but part of me wanted to be just like him. I was angry that people around town seemed to speak in hushed whispers whenever his name came up, and I didn't know whether to defend him or pour gas on the fire. I felt like I was swinging in the dark at an unknown enemy, and the slow burn of liquor felt like home.

But for some reason, Cameron Bastian always reached out

to me with kindness, which seemed to confuse a lot of people, me included, because we had absolutely nothing in common. We met in driver's training class, the summer of our sophomore year. He followed all of the rules, and I followed none of them. He aced the final driving test, and I had to retake it. Cam was the direct opposite of me in almost every conceivable way. He was an All-State Wide Receiver on the varsity football team, and was nominated to represent our class at Homecoming all four years of high school! Although he was a good student and inexplicably charismatic to the point of being a cliché, the truth is that he was popular for all the right reasons.

I remember the time he scored the winning touchdown against our biggest rivals on a Friday night under the bright stadium, lights. Later that same evening, he came to my defense in a little confrontation I had walked into with a few guys from the other school. I had been walking to my car and they were parked beside me, spitting chewing tobacco extremely close to my Jeep Cherokee. I don't remember exactly what I said to start it, but I realized rather quickly that I was in over my head trying to fight all three of them. All of a sudden, Cam mysteriously appeared, seemingly out of nowhere and literally throwing them back toward their truck. He helped me up and asked if I was okay. "Yeah," I said, looking at my one true friend. "I am now."

But the reason I loved Cam had nothing to do with his accolades or charisma and everything to do with a sincere joy that he possessed from the inside out. He lived out his faith with an unapologetic reverence. It was not uncommon for me to find him alone in his room in deep prayer, or reading his bible. He was always inviting me to his Youth Group at church, but I had better things to do. Like drink.

The object of Cameron's earthly affection was the excruciatingly beautiful Sierra. They met the summer of our junior year when they both worked as lifeguards at the community pool. I spent most of my summer hanging out there, baking in the sun and trying to get noticed by the flock of teen girls who lingered around Cam's lifeguard station.

Sierra was captivating from the first day I met her. While everyone else was scurrying to find shelter from the sudden rainstorm, she walked slowly against the wind. Children evacuated the community pool and ran toward the locker rooms, but Sierra held her hands out as if to collect the rain drops. Her toes were painted bright red, adding color to the invasive gray. I wondered aloud about her, and one of our classmates responded, "Yeah, that's Sierra. She just moved here." It was unclear at the time, from where she had moved, or why. Years later, I would learn that she never knew her father, and that her mom died of cancer at a young age.

Sierra was raised in Atlanta for most of her life, spending many of her formative years with distant relatives. The summer of our junior year she moved here to live with her grandfather on the south side of town. He lived in an old farmhouse, and cultivated old-fashioned values within her.

She was an introvert, but every time we saw her, she had a smile on her face. She used to clean the pool with all of her energy, while nearly every guy within eyesight would be rendered dysfunctional through frozen observation. Cam used to ignore the swimmers in the deep end, focusing his eyes like a laser on the gorgeous brunette in the red swimsuit.

Cam pursued Sierra relentlessly that summer. He was obsessed with her. He gave me a ride home from the pool almost every night, and his eyes would glaze over as he told me, "One day, I swear to God, I'm gonna marry that girl." And I knew he was right. I knew this because Cam *always* got what he wanted. He was the golden child with the perfect tan and the Brad Pitt hair, and I…was more like Brad Pitt's invisible brother.

It wasn't until the homecoming dance later that year that

Cameron finally apprehended Sierra. They had become friends over the summer, but she was slow to move into any commitment. I remember walking in to the crowded gym as we scanned the dance floor, Cam whispered to me, "Jordan, I'm going to ask Sierra out tonight and I'm not leaving until she dances with me!"

I preferred to stand against the wall in my usual anonymity. Although everything inside me wished I belonged out on the dance floor with the popular kids, I had assumed my natural position in the shadows. I would nod my head to the beat of the songs, but I did not know the words. I found safety in the refuge of my Styrofoam cup of artificial cherry punch.

"Hey, Jordan…do you want to dance with me?" I almost spilled my drink over the surprise of a familiar voice behind me.

I swiveled around behind and faced Sierra as she stood in the glow of flickering lights glittering like a star in an otherwise empty sky. I shook my head. Absolutely, positively, unequivocally, NO. "Come on!" she cajoled. "There's only a few more songs, and I'll teach you some of my moves!" As she said this, she cut beside me with her version of the electric slide, and I stood paralyzed before her. And once again, Cam came to my rescue

"There you are!" he said. Sierra pointed at me and responded, "I'm just trying to get this wallflower to leave his comfort zone and join the party!" Cameron agreed, "Yeah, Jordan, come on man!" I steadfastly shook my head like a shy, petulant child.

I watched Cameron lead Sierra by the hand to the center of the dance floor. As the music continued, he leaned into her ear and spoke softly. Sierra stopped moving and stood intentionally still while he continued to lean toward her. And after what seemed like an eternity, she smiled. She nodded her head and wrapped her arms around him like she was clinging to a life preserver in a stormy sea.

Leaving the Light On

The more we got to know Sierra, the more it became clear that Cameron was not alone in his affections for her. She was universally adored by a large circle of friends, and treated with honor by almost everyone in our school. She had a presence that was impossible to ignore and had a way of wooing you with her southern charm. It was to nobody's surprise that she swept Cam off his feet with one dance; it was as if she held some kind of kryptonite over every guy in our graduating class. Although her physical beauty was obvious, it was the inner beauty that seemed to shine the brightest. She was genuinely sensitive, in equal measure: a harsh word could shatter her spirit, but her eyes were always searching for the otherwise overlooked. "I'll leave the light on for you!" she would say to people, which inferred her willingness to accept anyone, anywhere, at any time, all hours of the day. When Sierra said she'd "leave the light on for you," it meant you could knock on her door even in the middle of the night and she would welcome you in with open arms, put on a pot of coffee, sit down, and listen.

The summer after our high school graduation, Sierra's grandfather passed away, leaving his beloved granddaughter behind a rickety old farmhouse about ten miles outside of town. Sierra converted it into a charming home, with light blue shutters. On more than one occasion, I would find myself stumbling toward the front door of her house, where she would be entertaining a room full of friends. Cam was always the center of attention, usually telling a self-deprecating story about growing up the youngest of six radiant children in an otherwise perfect existence. Out of the corner of my eye, I could see Sierra's gaze fixated on me, easing my way toward the light. In the shadows, her silhouette emerged like a statue of a southern belle, Sierra placed both hands on her hips, oozing with fake disappointment. "Jordan," she would say, "Where have you been?"

This, of course, was both a question and greeting. It had become our inside joke. Where have I been? She seemed to be the only one in the world who cared about my whereabouts, and after asking, she would wait intentionally for an honest answer. "I've been up to no good, Sierra," I would say. Every. Single. Time.

When All Else Fails

Despite getting several scholarship opportunities across the country, Cameron opted to stay close to home and play football at nearby Bridgeport University. It was a smaller school, known more for academics than athletics. This suited Cam just fine, because he always wanted to pursue a career in Public Administration. To be honest, I always thought he would emerge as the mayor of our city, or Governor of South Carolina. But Cam just wanted to live a simple life in Charleston. He never cared about the accolades or trophies he'd accumulated throughout the years. It just seemed like the more he avoided the spotlight, the more it found him.

On the weekends, we all used to pile into Sierra's Volkswagen and drive to watch Cameron play home games at the stadium on campus. Those were some of the happiest memories of my life: all of us there together, huddled in the crowd in the stands, with Sierra screaming her lungs out for her mighty warrior on the astroturf. I used to marvel at the vein in her neck, throbbing for air as she cheered for Cam with all of her soul. Her long, dark hair would be tucked back behind her ear, and her summer dress would modestly cover her tan shoulders. Sierra always wore colorful summer dresses, no matter the time of year, And even after the day she stepped on a black snake in the backyard trying to chase a hummingbird, she was usually barefoot, her toes sparkling with fifty shades of red ruby toenail polish.

But everything changed in the last game of the season in Cam's sophomore year, and After taking a hard tackle, Cam seemed to be limping. He looked over at the sideline, however, and waved off the substitution. Even though Bridgeport was up by three touchdowns, Cameron wanted to finish the game. As they neared the goal line, the quarterback called for pass to Cam in the corner of the end zone. A few seconds later, the football was hurled over his head, and Cam leaped to catch it. The pass was incomplete and Cameron landed awkwardly as his left knee buckled. He rolled over on his back and did not get up. We watched from the bleacher seats as the crowd hushed.

Sierra just put her hands over her eyes, as if to pray. She was not irrational, or emotional. She just stood there silently nodding. I expected her to rush out onto the field to Cam's side, but something kept her securely planted on the sideline. To this day, I don't know exactly why she was nodding, but at the time it seemed to me that she knew his football career was finished. When the team doctors arrived on the field and motioned for the cart, a hush came over the stadium. Cameron was carted off the field with a career-ending knee injury. His scholarship was therefore rescinded, and he would never play another down of football for his rest of his life.

As for me, college was never my cup of tea. I had enrolled at the local community college for a few semesters, but I struggled to see the point in any of it. I would never have the financial resources to transfer into a university, and just like in high school, my grades in college reflected my indifference. Besides, I could make more money in one summer hauling lumber to the Upstate Coalition than I ever would make in three years at the foundry where my dad had worked. I found a rhythm running the chainsaw and slicing the wood to custom pieces, collecting just enough cash to pay for my own apartment near Folly Beach.

Although I was never a scholastic achiever, I was an avid reader. I inhaled as many books as I could, often spending hours at a time over literary classics. I was a reclusive learner, getting drunk with Leo Tolstoy and F. Scott Fitzgerald, finding my own identity in the fictional characters portrayed.

One Friday evening after work, I stopped by our friendly, neighborhood dive bar. I had gotten to know Angie, the bartender, fairly well, and she always asked about my day. I attacked the free peanuts and chased the salt with a few glasses of beer. It was enough to elevate my blood alcohol level past the legal limit, apparently. Two miles down the road, a state trooper flashed his lights, and I would spend the weekend in jail.

Whereas most of my friends had gone away to college, Sierra stayed home to work at the elementary school near her house. She had spent three years volunteering with the special needs classroom, and eventually was offered a rewarding job doing what she loved to do: working as a teaching assistant to autistic children. We were all elated for her, because she had found so many fulfillments in dedicating her life to serve children.

I was always jealous of Cameron and Sierra. It wasn't the romantic chemistry that I envied, it was their spiritual energy. They both seemed to possess a faith that I could not resonate with, and a grace that I felt unworthy to receive. It was in the tender way they looked at each other, in the way they volunteered at the local soup kitchen every year. I watched the way they would interact with otherwise overlooked people or outcasts, like me. Why were they so unconditionally kind to me? I never understood what Cam saw in me, but over the years he had been my truest, and really my only, friend. And Sierra loved me because Cam loved me. And I think I loved them both too. I say "I think" here because, if I were to stop and be completely honest with myself, I'm not even sure if I know what love is.

Several months later, I had picked up my second DUI in the same year. By that time, I had gotten to know the local cops pretty well. I wasn't obnoxious, necessarily. Well… maybe I was just a little. After being held for 48 hours at the county jail, I was looking at spending a few weeks more. But I was surprised to have an officer unlock my door. "Let's go, Winter. You've been bailed out. Again." He placed an emphasis on "again." I walked down the hall, collected my original clothes, and searched my pockets for whatever cash I had left. I looked up from my pockets and saw Cam standing there quietly. He didn't say anything, just waited for me to walk toward his open arms. Once again, he had come to the rescue.

That night we drove to the beach, hardly saying a word during the ride. I could tell that Cameron was disappointed in me, and I was quite disappointed in myself as well. Little did I know that shame had already crept into my soul, and began to carve away at my identity. I was becoming my father, and everyone was thinking the same thing: this road will only lead to destruction.

Cam parked his truck in the vacant parking lot across the street from an otherwise desolate beach. In the distance, I saw the flickering of a bonfire, and I knew Sierra had been there for a few hours, waiting for us. There was a full moon that evening, and the reflection off the water provided just the right landscape to see her clearly. She was sitting in her summer dress, just watching the fire. However beautiful the scenery was, I could tell that something was heavy in the air.

"Sorry it took us so long," Cam said to her. "The cops gave me a hard time about getting Jordan out of jail. It seems they wanted to lock him up for a while this time." Sierra stood up and came over to sit beside me. This time she didn't ask the familiar, "Jordan, where have you been?" She already knew: I'd been up to no good.

I was grateful to Cameron for paying for my bail, and tried to offer him what little cash I had. As I suspected he would, he seemed oblivious to the gesture, and deeply focused on his valid concern. "Jordan... I love you, man, but you've got to make some serious changes in your life. This life you're living now isn't working; it's eating your present and stealing your future. I want to be the kind of friend that will call you out and lift you up." I didn't respond, just stared into the fire until my eyes began to silently water. Cameron continued, "But at the end of the day, it's your choice how you want to live or die."

Sierra remained quiet, content to hold sacred space for serious reflection. I did not feel judged or coerced. I could tell they both truly cared about me. They had become like the only family I knew.

I stood up to respond, but my words were scattered. "I don't know what to do with my life, to be honest. I mean, I don't have money for school. I was never a good student. I have no future outside of chopping wood or working at the foundry." I began to think about what my life would look like ten years from that moment. "Is this it? There's got to be more to life than just 'school, work, drink, die.' Apparently that's all my dad saw for his life, and he was right."

That night, we sat on the beach and talked for hours. Although we had not stacked a large pile of wood, the bonfire lasted the entire night. Under the stars, beside the rolling waves and smoldering fire, we reminisced, talking about middle school and lifeguard rescues and school suspensions, and then the talk turned to future plans.

"Jordan," Cam said intently. "I brought you out here to ask you something." Sierra did not act interested or surprised, which is how I could tell she already knew what he wanted to discuss. Clearly, they had rehearsed this ahead of time, and she was supportive of whatever was coming. I shrugged and fixed my eyes intently on Cam as he continued. "As you know, I lost my athletic scholarship after my knee injury, and unfortunately, I can't afford to pay for the rest of my tuition without it. I've been thinking about this a lot, and I believe it's God's will… I've decided to enlist in the Army for a four-year term. I absolutely need this opportunity because the GI Bill will subsequently pay for the rest of my college education."

This, of course, was not the conversation I was expecting. We had never even had a conversation about the military, let alone enrolling, and now he was about to fly to the other side of the world and fight in a war! Before I could respond or ask countless questions, he continued, "And I want you to enlist with me."

I couldn't believe my ears! Here I was, still hung over from a weekend of front porch, drinking in my underwear, and he wants to put a machine gun in my hands? "Are you serious? Cam, I can't be trusted behind the wheel of a car, let alone behind the trigger of an AK-47!"

Sierra smiled with assurance and finally spoke up. "Jordan, you can go and keep Cameron safe for me! You two have always been the best of friends... How could you ever live without each other?" She took a long stick and poked at the fire, as sparks flew upward. My initial hesitation was not backed with a credible reason. Every objection I presented was soundly defeated as Cameron and Sierra presented the reality: I had very little holding me to Charleston. The benefits of seeing the world and combat pay provided more options for my future, and the emphasis seemed to be on reward, not risk.

For the next few hours, the three of us talked in depth about the possibility of our enlistment. There were so many questions, but all of the other options seemed to be diminishing. The more I thought about it, the more my mind began to accept the concept of my imminent departure with Cam. He had already enlisted and made plans to leave for Boot Camp six weeks later, which only left for me with a short window of time to get my butt into shape, physically and emotionally.

In the distance, the orange sky began to catch on fire as the sun began to rise over the eastern horizon. We had talked ourselves to near sleep, and finally hushed to watch the sunrise over the crashing waves. And here we stood: three best friends, discussing the closing of one chapter and the beginning of another. The weeks ahead would initiate the deconstruction of our foundations, and the recapitulation of a love story rooted in nuclear grace.

Chapter 2

Exodus to the Promised Land

Six weeks had passed since that night on the beach. As word began to spread around town, acquaintances suddenly became "friends," and I was awakened to the progressive expressions of patriotism. My eyes were gradually opened to the number of front porches with American flags waving so proudly in the South Carolina breeze. Even in my morning run along Folly Beach, I began to gain a confidence not yet realized. My stamina improved, and I even quit smoking. But then again, I only smoked when I was drinking... so, pretty much all the time.

I put in my notice at the lumber yard, but it went fairly unnoticed. Such was the story of my life. Ever since middle school when I didn't receive one vote for my high school class nomination, I had evolved into a ghost with no shadow, a face with no name. After my dad went to prison, no sooner than the cell had barely locked behind him that my mother began to immediately search for his replacement, and I assumed the shell of house that was not a home for a body that had no soul.

The only time I felt visible was in the presence of Sierra. I loved when she opened her door and welcomed me into her home. I loved the culture we unintentionally created over the years of her asking about my whereabouts and my familiar refrain: *I've been up to no good.* And despite Cameron's deliberate attempts to honor my presence in a crowded room, the times I felt the most ignored were when he was in the circumference. His personality seemed to hijack the attention of everyone, like the drum beat of an African village and the magnetic call of the tribe.

In the weeks leading up to our simultaneous departure for basic training at Fort Jackson in Columbia, Cam began to be even more heralded as the ultimate hometown celebrity warrior. It seemed there was an optimistic light in his eyes that revived patriotism in a town that had grown weary of the Obama Administration, or the white noise of active combat on the other side of the world.

He was sensitive to my feelings, however, and Cameron quickly pointed people to recognize his "best man" standing beside him. In classic southern hospitality, people would politely nod to me as if to say, 'Bless your heart!' and refocus their attention on Cameron. I got used to the heart blessings and the plastic dispositions of insincerity. I knew that my heart was not blessed; rather, it was broken. The brokenness was not because of love lost, but because it had never been found in the first place. I felt an inability to empathize with others who were grieving, or infatuated with romantic attraction. My high school guidance counselor once told me regarding love, "It's impossible to lose something you never had in the first place."

As a child, I never had the luxury of witnessing a man's demonstration of love for a woman. My dad used to beat my mom every weekend, and in return she would be gone for weeks on end. I had heard rumors of her whereabouts and whatnots with so-and-so on the other side of the tracks, and by the time my mother had remarried, I had become emotionally absent. My departure was a coping mechanism for the abandonment I had already felt at an early age, and my self-medication included thoughts of suicide, fantasies of swimming with sharks, running with bulls, and drinking poison until the some glad morning when I'd fly away.

The closest I had ever felt to being in love was the simple witness of the invisible voltage between Sierra and Cameron. I didn't know it then, but I see now that I was envious of the way she looked at him. As he became increasingly popular around our community, Cam seemed to shine like the North Star in a universe of black holes and gravitational pulls into oblivion. He didn't ask for attention, and yet he got it everywhere he went, and he deserved it. Sierra used to gaze lovingly at him like a star-crossed lover with x-ray vision. There was an inexplicable intensity in the way she seemed to undress him with her eyes, and could connect directly to his soul. It seemed as if she didn't care if there were anyone else in the room, she had an insatiable immodesty to the way she desired him.

I wanted someone to look at me like that. I had never felt the touch of a woman, or the unconditional embrace of committed love. I used to dream about traveling to exotic destinations, and perhaps finding a Sierra of my own. I wondered if I was too dysfunctional to be in a relationship, and maybe the Army could remedy my lack of discipline and commitment.

So I hit the free weights like a hammer to a nail, and pushed myself to the limits of physical ability. I did nothing in moderation, but rather everything in the extreme. My diet changed, my habits were broken. I didn't just jog; I sprinted at full speed. It was all or nothing, for me. I really wanted to change my ways, and break my cycles of addiction to the affirmation of others. I cut out any expressions of codependency. I vowed from now on that my new addiction would be freedom. I devoted every waking moment to the self-discipline of sobriety and focused energy on the deconstruction of unhealthy patterns of self-destruction. I replaced bad habits with good ones, and fought hard to pick myself up by my own boot straps, (as my dad used to say). This worked for a while, but time would reveal that I was, in fact, powerless.

I even tried to wake up early enough to attend church with Sierra and Cam. This was a big stretch for me, because I have always had a love/hate relationship with God. He seemed to be the

Sovereign King whom I held responsible for the train wreck that was my parents' marriage. And by fourth grade, I had dismissed the flannel graph presentations at Sunday school, chalking up the Triune God-head as just another fictitious character meant to discourage children from misbehaving. I found God to be suspiciously like Santa Claus, who was known for making lists and checking it twice to see if I'd been naughty or nice. And despite my best efforts to be nice, I always seemed to get a stocking full of bull manure for Christmas.

I didn't know their songs. I wanted to sing along with the chorus, but I just listened. Cam used to close his eyes and sometimes even raise his hand toward heaven during the worship, as if he were giving God a high-five. I once wore a T-shirt that said, "Jesus is my homeboy" across the front, which deeply upset Cam, who called it "sacrilegious." I didn't know what sacrilege was, but I wanted to have the kind of relationship with God that wouldn't mind me referring to his son as my homeboy or bro. Sierra, however, used to sing the hymns with the intensity of a hungry lioness, clearly believing in the words on the screen: "A thousand times I've failed, and your mercy remains. If I stumble again, still I'm caught by your grace... Everlasting."

But my invisibility was never more excruciatingly obvious than the morning of our simultaneous departure for Basic Training. I had a few bags all packed and ready to go and had agreed to meet Cameron at the Greyhound bus station, where we were scheduled to depart at noon. I had already arranged to have my power shut off, so I just locked up my apartment and walked the several blocks to the center of town. I had nobody to call, and there were no sad goodbyes. Even my mom hadn't bothered to see me off. I saw that she had marked the day on her calendar, but evidently she forgot about it. As I walked to the bus station, I carried virtually all of my possessions in two bags, and I began to prepare myself mentally for the initiation of a new chapter.

As I neared closer to the bus station, I was distracted by the commotion of a large crowd assembled in the grass outside the building. I immediately recognized some familiar faces, and upon closer inspection, I saw Cam surrounded by friends and family members. It seemed to be his going away party, with the electricity of a flash mob on steroids. His mom was wearing oversized sunglasses to shield her tears, and his father was wearing an American flag tee shirt. The whole scene was consistent with what I'd come to expect, and it was only fitting that I was outside the circle, looking in.

While the crowd gathered to see Cam's departure, I sat across the grass on a park bench and pulled out a notebook. Although we had discussed my plans to enlist in the Army, my mother never really seemed to care. I felt anger and sadness, resentment and love. The truth lives in the paradox, I supposed. I suddenly felt overcome with sentiment and decided to write her a goodbye letter

"Dear Mom,

I'm leaving this morning for basic training with the Army. For the next six weeks, I'll be at Fort Jackson in Columbia. You can write to me there if you want to. I hope you will. But I just wanted to let you know that I am really trying to make some changes in my life, and I want to make you proud. I'm sorry if I haven't kept in touch, and I regret that we hardly ever talk anymore."

The sound of a train whistle interrupted my conclusion to the letter, which unfortunately I never finished or sent. I shoved my notebook back into my bag and started to walk toward the silver bus that was idling in front of the brick building. By now, the high noon sun had chased away whatever morning fog had lingered. Cam tore himself loose from the crowd and began to make his way toward the line of travelers waiting to climb into the bus.

I could hear them all shouting various sentiments:"Goodbye," "We love you!" "Keep in touch, buddy!" But when Cam saw me standing in line, he simply cut past everyone else and joined me. "There you are!" Cam said as he stood beside me and bumped my fist with his own. "I thought maybe you had a change of heart and decided to go AWOL before the first day!"

He was standing in the direct line of harsh, glaring sunlight, which made it impossible to see him clearly. I squinted in his direction and said, "I've been sitting over there on that bench for the last half hour, writing a letter." The line moved slowly toward the stairs of the bus. Cam seemed intrigued. "Who were you writing a letter to, and what did it say?" I shrugged dismissively and said, "To nobody. And it said nothing."

Just then I saw Sierra walking toward us. She was carrying a basket, walking barefoot of course. I could immediately see that she had been crying, her mascara-streaked tears running down her cheeks. Later, I found out that she had stayed up all night trying to beg Cam to change his mind and stay home, but he wouldn't back down. He wanted to finish his education. So here she stood before us, trembling with sadness.

"I'm not going to say goodbye, but I want you to fare well. And God speed you to return back to me. I want both of you to come home to me tomorrow, and if not tomorrow, then the next day, and if you can't return the next day, then I will keep praying for your return every single morning until we're all together again!" She clutched Cameron's right arm to the point of nearly cutting off circulation, making it obvious that she was afraid to navigate through life without him, didn't want to even imagine a life without him. Then she turned to face us both once more and said, "I'll leave the light on for you," with trembling lips.

Sierra held out her basket, revealing a stockpile of chocolate chip cookies. It wasn't carefully thought out, but it was the thought that counts. We couldn't take the whole basket with us, so we each took a stack of her homemade delights, and climbed onto the bus. The cookies were devoured by the time we put our seatbelts on.

Cam sat directly beside me in the aisle seat. I pressed my face against the window. Despite the fact that the glass windows were tinted, Sierra somehow could see where we were sitting. She stood alone on the sidewalk, sunburn slowly spreading across her rosy cheeks. She did not wave. She simply stood there, motionless, staring in our direction like a sad puppy. I looked over at Cam and he shook his head and mumbled, "They don't make 'em like her anymore. She's one of a kind," he said.

Deconstruction and Resurrection

I had always heard that the first half of basic training is the intentional demolition of a soldier's psyche, with the strategy to recapitulate his entire being. The physical, mental, and psychological anguish was meant to purposefully break us down only to build us up, the character of a man so we could become killing machines, only with integrity and patriotism.

My first observation of this came upon our arrival to Fort Jackson. The late September sun had set in Columbia, South Carolina, leaving unprecedented heat waves. Immediately stepping off the air-conditioned bus, the inferno of blazing rage assaulted our cognition. We were politely greeted by the ominous screaming of a drill instructor that seemed to be a bit uptight about our late arrival, blaming the passengers as if we had some disrespectful agenda, or had been the ones driving the bus. I could not comprehend or discern what exactly he was screaming about, but we were all demanded to march behind the building, where we were sectioned off in alphabetical order. This was the last time I saw Cameron for the next three weeks.

The unexpected separation from Cam was disconcerting, because our military recruiter had led us to believe we would serve our time in basic training together, literally side by side. That was not the first time, or the last, that we would be lied to by our government. Instead, I was assigned to the bottom bunk of a crammed dormitory on the east end of the base. I would find out later that Cam's group had been assigned to the opposite spectrum of the campus. This would explain why our paths would not cross for three of the most grueling weeks of my life.

The stories of basic training are consistent with my experience. I had mentally prepared myself for the verbal assaulting of raging lunatics disguised as officers. They did not scare me, and I welcomed the spewing of hate. In some twisted way, it felt good. Perhaps it was the self-hatred for myself I had always carried, or my desire to be punished for my having been born into a dysfunctional family, but whatever the reason, I embraced the insults.

"Winter!" screamed the drill instructor. "Stop tip-toeing around like a limp-wristed princess and step into your manhood!"

This verbal assault did nothing to my egocentric impulse. As a matter of fact, I probably agreed that I lacked the testosterone to stand out in this culture of black coffee and gun smoke, and I made no effort to respond. "Sir, yes, sir!" I screamed. In my mind I was thinking, *tell me something I don't already know.* I had been verbally beaten down for years. But for whatever reason, I was a glutton for punishment. Everything I said was wrong. If I showed initiative in answering rhetorical questions, I was criticized for being outspoken. If I stayed quiet, my drill instructor screamed at me to have the guts to speak up. Everything I did seemed to be in error, and by the second week of Basic Training, I was about ready to stab my drill instructor in the face and run back to Charleston to resume my life cutting lumber.

Basic training was my first introduction to the United States campaign to shock and awe. It was a violent wake up from the fantasy I had imagined when we originally dreamed of enlisting. Seeing the world and excellent pay seemed to camouflage a sinister evil. I was quickly disillusioned and tempted to run away. Or at the very least, eat peanuts and drink beer.

After three weeks, I had begun to feel like I was locked in the basement of hades, forced to eat concrete poison and drink from the cup of hate, I'd had enough. It seemed like an eternity had passed since Cam and I used to surf at Folly Beach and toss a Frisbee. I had grown physically exhausted and sick, throwing up the disgusting mess hall food in the dry heaving of torturous repetitions. Climbing walls were followed by eight-mile runs in the melting sun, only to be repeated in the afternoon. Requests for water were met with additional pushups, and there were no comforting words of affirmation.

On one particularly blazing afternoon, I collapsed while running the obstacle course. My head began to spin and I was losing consciousness and collapsed to the ground. In a matter of seconds, my drill instructor had bended to one knee, and was screaming in my face. I can honestly say that if I were in the vicinity of a loaded weapon, I would have shot him without apology. But I didn't have the emotional or physical strength to respond, and instead lay motionless staring across the camp yard and stare as the other soldiers continued their regimen.

My drill instructor began to intentionally verbally assault me, which is meant to inflict psychological trauma. He unleashed a litany of criticism, beginning with my "loose" mother, calling her every curse word available from his dictionary of insults, but ironically, it did not faze me in the least or upset me, since I thought it was probably true. After all, my mother *had* left me. She was notorious for her absence and neglect. She'd been the enabling reinforcement of the town drunk, a pill-popping drug addict who cared neither for herself nor her only child. All of these things were true.

Despite my drill instructor's saliva spraying my face and his deafening roar to get up and continue running, I heard nothing but white noise. I was caught up in a temporary state of disassociation (my therapist would one day refer to this psychological phenomenon as the ' fugue state'), as if I were having an out-of-body experience. In that moment, it almost felt like I was hovering above the whole scene, and all of a sudden, I caught a glimpse of Cam.

He was on the other side of the yard, participating in a group exercise, physically carrying a weaker member of his squad. They had been assigned the duty of retrieving a wounded soldier and bringing him to safety... and there was Cam, being a hero. I watched him closely as his arms trembled to lift his overweight companion and bring him across the wall to the finishing point.

In a matter of a few seconds, I snapped out of my state of unconsciousness. I climbed to my feet and started running with everything I had. But this time, I ran like Forrest Gump across that Alabama football field, at full speed! I was rejuvenated and inspired, both from personal conviction and an inward desire to reach my potential. Cameron had sparked me with the fuel to not give up, and I wanted so desperately to be like him.

A few days later, I finally caught up to Cameron during a short window of free time. He had just gotten off the phone with his mother, and saw me from across the mess hall. Even in the few weeks of our separation, I could already see a difference in his chiseled features. His deltoids popped out of his t-shirt, and his posture had improved. He walked tall and proud, revealing broad shoulders and a steady, determined gaze. He nodded and walked toward me. "I've been looking for you everywhere, Jordan! How are you holding up?" I paused, and then admitted, "Honestly, it's been brutal, man. I almost went postal last week. I've about had it with this whole scene."

We sat down at a nearby vacant table, and I continued talking. "I mean, seriously... who would sign up voluntarily to get screamed at and beat up and kicked and then shot at by people you don't even know?"

Cam laughed at my logical question, and seemed to agree. "I know, man," he said. "And believe me; I've had a few moments of reconsideration myself. And sometimes I regret having talked you into coming with me." Cameron opened a plastic bottle of water and took a sip. In a moment of reflection, he seemed to be wrestling with words of encouragement. "But if we give up now, Jordan... if we give up now, there is no redemption. We have to keep going."

We sat together in the evening hours, catching up on the past three weeks of each other's particular horrific traumas. It was absolutely brutal to hear Cameron describe the way his fellow squad members were betraying each other, stealing food and fighting. Apparently at one point, Cam broke up a knife fight between two soldiers, and could have been severely wounded. But those situations explained why Cam was a beloved, strong leader. He intervened without any cause or concern for himself, and just always wanted to restore peace.

The second half of our basic training was the intentional inverse of the first half. Instead of the verbal assaults and tearing down, the Army officers were trying to rebuild the psychological framework into the complete soldier. Self-confidence was the chief objective, and our scandalous mothers now became respectable women for whom we were defending our country.

The transformation of my physical body was nothing short of miraculous. I had come into Fort Jackson with a modest profile, and the stamina of an amateur athlete. But as a result of the onslaught of relentless self-discipline, the repetitions produced muscles that I didn't even know existed! I had lost body fat, and gained lean muscle. I could feel my arms throbbing as I lay in bed each night, exhausted. And most importantly, I gained a new self-confidence in overcoming obstacles.

Cam and I had the luxury of spending the final week of boot camp together. He too, had gained an enormous amount of muscle.

Whereas he had always been athletic and strong, there was a new swagger in his eyes, and he was earning the respect of our peers for more than just his personality. He was chiseled and capable of destroying a man with his bare hands. And on more than one occasion, he would have that opportunity.

By the time we graduated from basic training, I had almost forgotten about my former way of living back on Folly Beach. I resented how lazy I had lived most of my life so far. I couldn't believe how much time I wasted trying to claw my way into the circle of acceptance and fighting, and how much money I spent on alcohol. For the first time in my life, I had accomplished something, and when I lined up with the other men under the overcast sky, I felt (at least for a moment) a connection to a Higher Power. I wanted to give God a high five.

At the conclusion of the ceremony, the military officials brought out a children's choir from a village in Tanzania. They were a tightly knit semicircle of bright yellow, green, and orange against dark skin and ivory-white teeth. From the third row of my unit, I locked eyes on one little boy who sang with an exceptionally expressive gusto:

> "His eye is on the sparrow, and I know He watches me..."

I glanced over at Cam, who had simultaneously been looking at me. He nodded his head, and I smiled. For the first time in a long time, I felt a sense of wholeness and I wanted it to last forever. I didn't actually want to go overseas into active combat, or let the sound of screaming children and explosions drown out the harmony of all creation, groaning for redemption. And this was a song I could finally sing. I knew this chorus, and I joined right in there.

Chapter 3

Land of the Free, Home of the Brave

Thunder rolled and lightning slammed into the wall of heat waving through the Carolina coast. Record temperatures had caused widespread panic as the Indian summer raged on into late September. The heat lightning exploded in the horizon, even as the power lines failed to radiate any shimmer. Long after the clouds hid the sun away, images and shadows were painted in brilliant flashes. Here in a moment, then gone. Even the overlap of time between Basic Training and our departure for our advanced individual training seemed like the blink of an eye. It was the shortest two weeks of my life.

From a distance, I could see Sierra's house glowing in the midnight rain. The candles illuminated an open table from within, and I could see I was late to the party. Although it was an informal gathering, this was not the kind of invitation I would have passed up. Several cars lined the driveway and along the country roadway as I walked closer. Hard, heavy raindrops soaked me from the upside down, and my heart was restless from the inside out. I was leaving for Iraq in the morning, and I had come to say goodbye.

True, I had lingered over a few too many drinks. By my 22nd birthday, I had built up quite a huge bar tab with Angie, who knew I was good for it. Her boyfriend Brandon bought me a few drinks, and I had previously arranged for a taxi to transport me to the after-party, so I gave myself permission to get lost with my friends Jim (Beam) and Jack (Daniels). But it was also true that I knew I was afraid of the imminent future, and the reality of active combat had me mortified. One more drink, one more song on the jukebox, one more borrowed quarter to hear Bruce Springsteen crooning about the Glory Days - anything to make time slow down.

Stumbling in the dark toward the flickering light, I approached the front steps and listened to the music on the inside. Before I knocked on the door, I lingered in the rain for a few more seconds. Inside I could hear laughter and music and the melody of the circle of acceptance. I could smell the aroma of home cooking, and even as the thunder hummed in the distance, I could hear my heart beating. Maybe it was the alcohol, or the chemical romance of a thousand emotions colliding, but I was struggling to identify the source of the sentimentality. This was a sacred sadness, and I did not want to leave this porch.

I raised my fist to knock, but just as I was about to make contact, the door magically swung open.

"Where have you been, Jordan?" Sierra stood in the doorway with one hand on her hip, the other hand holding a roman candle. She arched a scowling eyebrow and tried her best to act as my disapproving mother. But even her best effort to look intimidating was as disarming as a puppy under a Christmas tree. She looked me up and down and shook her head in pitiful disappointment. I tilted my head and shrugged, "I've been up to no good." She had grown accustomed to my familiar routine, and yet she slowly reached out with her open arm to greet me. I was dizzy from the drinking, and delirious to be welcomed inside. "I tried to leave the light on for you," she said. "But most of the candles are all burned out."

By this time, the runaway raindrops had begun to fall on her as well. Instead of immediately inviting me into the warmth of her

27

home and out of the rain, she stood outside the front door with me. While everyone else inside continued socializing, Sierra seemed content to stand in the rain with me for an awkward moment of silence. She put one hand over her candle to shield the flame from being extinguished. "Sit down for a minute, Jordan. I want to talk to you."

Sierra motioned for me to sit down on the front steps beside her. I followed her lead, preparing for a lecture about my residual self-destructive path, and how I needed to give my life to the Lord and get baptized or something. She looked at me, tucked her long hair back behind her ear, and said, "I need to ask you a favor. Will you do something for me?"

Obviously, this was a loaded question. It would depend on the legitimacy of her request, but we both knew that there was nothing I wouldn't do for her. Sierra was one of my closest friends. I loved her like a sister, a mother, a father, and a brother.

"What is it? You want me to go to church more often? Say a prayer with the chaplain or something? Oh, wait. Is this about my drinking? Because I was just blowing off some steam before we leave tomorrow..."

Sierra shook her head. Then she nodded. "No. Wait, yes. I mean… it's all of those things too, of course, but that's not what I wanted to talk with you about." Just then, the rain dripped from her hairline and caught the tip of the flame immediately extinguishing the candle. She looked down momentarily at the candle and then immediately back into my eyes.

"I wanted to ask you to keep a close eye on Cam for me." She said. I waited for her to continue, unsure as to what she meant. "I know he's a grown man and he can take care of himself, but I'm worried about him. He has such a big heart, and he can get himself in trouble by always trying to be the hero. You know, it's like… it's like he feels like it's his destiny or something. And so many times, he has been the rescuer, the messiah. I'm afraid that he has

28

begun to believe he's immortal and bulletproof." Sierra stood up, and I could see the outline of her face in the soft glow of candles from inside the living room window. Maybe it was just the rain, but I could have sworn there were legitimate tears streaming down her face.

I nodded, but didn't say anything at first. I could definitely see how she could have arrived at this conclusion, considering all the times Cam had rescued me. And once again, in my selective hearing, I was interpreting this request to be more about my carelessness than his cautiousness. "Of course I'll keep an eye on him, Sierra. Cam's my best friend, and he knows I've got his back. He'll be okay, I promise."

She was just about to respond when the front door opened. Sierra's cousin, Allie, stood in demand for our attention. "What are you guys doing out here in the rain? Come in here, the food is ready!" Sierra turned abruptly and went inside, walking past Allie, who stood frozen in the doorway, glaring down at me like a bouncer at a club. She had never liked me, although I never knew why, exactly. But that never bothered me because she drove a Volkswagen Beetle with a personalized plate, and I thought everything about her self-absorbed culture of cute was obnoxious. I winked at her sarcastically as I sauntered past her and muttered under my breath, "Thanks, precious."

Once inside the house, friends scattered around the living room and spilled out of the kitchen to warmly greet me. Cam was grunting beside the fireplace, trying to keep the flame alive. He was laughing at Ryan who proudly announced that he had once been an Eagle Scout, and referred to him as "Eagle" for the rest of the night. The laughter between the two of them seemed to quickly transition into back-and-forth bickering about the best way to keep the fire going, until Sierra finally walked bluntly toward the fireplace and squeezed a can of lighter fluid. "There," she said.

"Now you boys can stop flexing your muscles and get busy setting the table!"

Cam stood up and rolled his eyes with a smirk. His eyes caught mine and motioned for me to join him. I didn't mind helping in the kitchen, because I had obviously arrived just in time to eat a homemade meal. While Cameron and I were transporting hot plates of fried chicken and corn into the dining room, he asked me where I'd been.

"I've spent most of the night at The Alibi with Angie and Brandon, shootin' pool and tellin' lies," I said casually. "You know they won't let me get out of there without a few drinks." As we set down the plates and started setting the table, Cam seemed interested in hearing the rest of the story. "What lies?"

"Oh, you know. Just blowing smoke," I said. Cam shook his head. Although he must have known that I was just kidding around, he seemed serious. "No, Jordan, I don't know. What lies were you telling while you were blowing smoke and shooting pool?" Cam had a way of cutting to the chase with his conversations. He used to quote Mark Twain, who once said that if he had more time, he would have said less.

"Well, they were asking me if I was afraid of going off to Iraq," I said quietly. In that moment of sheer silence, I could hear the sound of rain pattering against the window over the kitchen sink. Cam must have been distracted by it too because he reached up to make sure the latch was secured. Then he turned back to me and asked, "What did you say?"

"I said no." I shrugged, casually.

Cameron set a bowl of bread on the counter and volleyed the response, "Are you?"

There have been plenty of times when Cam and I have blurred the lines between sarcasm and sincerity, but this was not one of those times. He was dead serious, as he waited for my authentic self to respond to the most direct of questions. Was I afraid of going into active combat? Did the thought of getting sprayed with the shrapnel of exploding pieces of metal into my body terrify me? At the heart of the question is the mystery of life and death and mortality and ever-elusive peace that transcends understanding.

"Yes," I admitted.

Cam nodded, as if he were relieved to hear my confession of fear. He sighed and hung his head in a moment of profound honesty. The shadows of flickering candles might have hidden the tears welling up in his eyes. "Me too," he confessed.

That evening turned out to be one of the most sacred memories I would carry throughout my entire life. Everything about it seemed to scream of primal authenticity. No lights, no music, no air-conditioned comfort or blenders or vacuums or amplified energy. Just spoken words, homemade food, good friends, and heartfelt laughter around the table. And at the center of it all sitting in her sundress, covering the delicate hurricane of love, was Sierra, shining in the flames of fading candles. She wholeheartedly adored every person around the table, especially the man sitting to her left. Cameron raised a glass to the unknown future and stood up to make a toast.

"In the words of the great prophet Jay Z," he said, "'May the best of our todays be the worst of our tomorrows.'"

Give Me Liberty Or Give Me Death

Several months had passed since our graduation from Basic Training. Cameron and I were simultaneously sent to advanced individual training, where we learned technical skills related to our imminent assignments in Baghdad. It was a grueling two months of learning telecommunications and tactical training for combat missions. On the other side of foundational training, Cam and I were both assigned to "11 Bravo Company" with the Army Infantry School, meaning we'd both be on the front lines of Operation Iraqi Freedom.

Walking through the airport in our military fatigues, Cameron and I were treated like royalty. Although the nation was divided over our military presence in the Middle East, there seemed to remain a high amount of respect given to new recruits. I walked beside Cam through the chaos of the Atlanta airport, scanning for confirmation of our departure time. We each carried a bag full of only the necessities, sporting identical buzz cuts to announce our status to other passengers as Army grunts.

We arrived a few minutes too early, so we stood against the wall and waited patiently. An elderly man offered us his seat as a gesture of honor. By now we were beginning to identify who the retired combat veterans were by their solidarity of spirit. I shook my head and said, "No, thank you, sir." The truth was, I was too anxious to sit down, and we were about to be seated for a very long time. Cam went off in search of a cup of coffee, while I leaned against the wall. On the television screen over our heads was a news story about further demonstrations of terrorism; the broadcast continued to replay the same images of smoke and fire, screaming and crying women and children, and video evidence of the carnage that had become our humanity. I wanted to vomit.

While I waited for his return, I thought about Cam. He was notoriously optimistic about our objective, and seemed to believe in the legacy of life, liberty, and the pursuit of happiness. He had been raised a patriot, and his father had been a decorated combat veteran from the Vietnam War. He always put his hand over his heart during the Star-Spangled Banner. "September 11th changed everything," he said. "It's one thing for them to hate us from a distance, but the minute they set foot on our soil and tried to destroy our country, we rose up and showed them what America is all about!"

In contrast with Cam's patriotism, I had struggled for most of my life to identify a passion for just about anything. However, I reasoned that if someone broke into my house, I'd probably pop a cap and crack a forty over his head. But until then, I didn't care. I had a hard time putting my hand over my heart and pledging "allegiance" to just about anything. And the larger the scope of our American government, the more disillusioned I was about submitting to the empire of greed and violence and peace through the sword.

Once we boarded the plane, I leaned against the window and looked out at the runway before us. Cam sat beside me and put on his headphones, and I knew within a few minutes he would be fast asleep. I was feeling sick with almost every possible symptom known to man, including (but not limited to) a migraine headache, upset stomach, and a growing sense of oppositional defiant disorder. The flight attendant reviewed the various ways to respond in case of a crash: to maintain a non-anxious presence, to just calmly apply your oxygen mask first and then assist other passengers politely. I lowered the shade over the window, rested my head against the glass, and closed my eyes.

The flight, although ridiculously uncomfortable, was otherwise uneventful. The overhead television played a few B-grade movies, including a movie about a notebook, a lady with Alzheimer's and her memoirs from her younger, more cohesive years. I decided that whoever wrote the script was cheesy, and that Hollywood had not yet developed a genre for romantic novels that do not always end with a happily ever after, with rainbows and kittens and unicorns. *What about my mom and dad? Where was their love story? Had they ever even had one?* The more I thought about it, the more I realized the only visible expression of true love that I had ever witnessed was the display of devotion between Sierra and Cameron, and I wondered if I would ever have the fortune of finding such joy for myself.

Chapter 4

From Boys to Men

The next six months were a horrific blur of confusion and chaos and all things unholy. It didn't take long for me to lose hope in any kind of redemption in all of this mess. Everything I had learned in advanced individual training was thrown out the window during our very first active combat mission. All the education, training, practice, and experience in the world can never prepare you for the massive adrenaline surge you face in this environment—the sounds of stray bullets and screaming children.

To make matters worse, Cameron and I were immediately separated according to alphabetical order, and he was stationed at another base with another assigned directive. Although we were able to catch up on rotating days off, it never seemed to satisfy the restlessness in my heart. I just wanted to go home. I wanted to go surfing, and sit around a bonfire under the South Carolina sky. But until then, my alarm clock would be the screaming alarm of a city in ruin, and the ashes of despair seemed to be my constant companion. Cameron had caught the attention of some of the officers of the Black Beret, a Special Forces elite category. They identified a few of the men in our unit as having the capacity to lead, and discussed the possibilities of continued training. Cameron had quickly achieved the respect and admiration of the men and women in his unit, and I even heard a story about his fearlessness in the wake of a bomb threat. While I was sitting at breakfast with two guys from Wisconsin (I was never very good at remembering names, but I could always remember where people were from) who described the scene in graphic detail:

"... A vehicle had slowed to a stop in front of a crowded marketplace. The driver abruptly exited the car and disappeared into the crowded streets." I set down my coffee mug and leaned in to hear more. "Everyone was in a panic, assuming a time bomb was about to detonate. I mean... you should have seen the look in the commanding officer's eyes when he screamed for backup. And that's when Cameron just walked up without hesitation. He seemed undaunted in the investigation, and volunteered to examine the scene without waiting for the command." According to the rest of the story, Cam had broken through the passenger side window with the butt of his gun and unlocked the door. He searched the vehicle for any sign of danger, and eventually found a wired box in the backseat under a blanket. The rest of the story further solidified the legendary fearlessness that Cameron had become known for. Although he was severely reprimanded by his commanding officer for violating procedural training, he was quickly celebrated by his peers. There is a thin line between truth and falsehood in the secondhand stories of sleepless soldiers.

It seemed like the only time I was able to see Cam was at the chapel service on base. Every Wednesday evening, there was a midweek service complete with a lengthy discussion and even communion after each gathering. I tried to attend as often as possible, but I think I was there more for the solidarity it brought among a room full of strangers searching for the common good and the hope of peace. And of course, the free coffee didn't hurt.

Our chaplain was a retired military officer who had gone back to Seminary to obtain his Divinity degree. He said he had felt a "calling" to return to the mission field, where men were so hungry for answers. I didn't like Chaplain Acheson at first, but as time went on, he would prove to be an invaluable resource during my stay in Baghdad. He always greeted me by first name, and when you're on the other side of the world, it feels good just to hear someone say your name.

On one particular gathering, he noticed my restlessness. From the back row, I must have been visibly frustrated with his teaching. I was constantly tapping my foot and chewing off my fingernails. Cam whispered for me to knock it off, but I didn't even realize that my crossed arms were communicating some disturbance from deep within. Chaplain Acheson had been talking about the Old Testament story of Job, and about all this really cryptic violence that happened to him. According to the oral tradition, Job was hit with an earthquake, lost all of his material possessions, and even his children were killed. All of this happened in just one day, and all of this, according to Chaplain Acheson, by the orchestration of an all-loving God.

During the coffee break after the teaching, I approached the chaplain with a litany of questions. "So let me get this straight. God is good and loving and kind, right?" I sarcastically asked. Chaplain Acheson unbuttoned the top button of his starched white shirt, a single bead of sweat slowly dripping from his forehead like a runaway freight train. He smiled and said, "I already know what you're going to ask… why would a loving God inflict all of these awful things on an innocent man…right?"

"Exactly." I nodded with more than a little enthusiasm. This whole God thing was terribly frustrating. In the Old Testament, he seemed to endorse genocide, and in the New Testament, he seemed to suddenly be a pacifist. And what about all of those contradictions? First, God says that nobody could see him and live. But then Chaplain Acheson talked about Moses, who was a "friend of God" and how he saw God face to face. I wanted to see God face to face, like Moses.

When I was a little boy, I went to church with my Aunt Tracy a few times. I was taught to pray to God because He is in control. So I prayed for my daddy to stop drinking, and for my parents to stop fighting. I had been taught that God was good, but then my dad went to prison and my mom emotionally disappeared. He didn't prove to be very good to me.

The chaplain went on to affirm the question, and said that this debate was an ancient "problem of evil" that theologians and philosophers had wrestled with for thousands of years. He didn't try to give me some cliché answers or dismissive responses, but rather, he recognized the tension of the story. He went on to describe the polarities between God's Sovereign Will and the freedom we have to respond however we want. "Some people choose to climb into airplanes and crash into the World Trade Center with their free will. Others choose to give their lives in service to others, like the firemen of September 11."

While we were walking home from church that evening, Cam seemed quieter than usual. He was listening to my frustrations and questions, but wasn't saying much back. It was obvious that although he was physically walking next to me, his mind was a million miles away. After walking in silence for a minute, I asked, "What's wrong?"

"I just want to go home, I guess. I don't know," he said. Considering how optimistic he had originally been about our mission in Iraq, it seemed completely out of character for Cam to be anxious to leave. I listened as he continued, "I was talking to Sierra the other day, and she's been having a hard time back in Charleston. They cut her hours at work, and it's been a financial struggle to make it on her own." We stopped at the drinking fountain in the front of the mess hall. While I leaned forward to take a sip, Cameron looked at his watch. "I've got to get back. I told her I'd call tonight." Then he disappeared around the corner and left me standing silently in the dirt road.

Jay DePoy

We're Not in Kansas Anymore

One of the chief responsibilities of our unit was to track down insurgents who were suspected to be living within a ten-mile radius of our base on the southwest side of Baghdad. Throughout basic training, we learned how to work as an offensive team in approaching ominous threats in civilian households. Although memorizing the various hand signals and codes and radio communication was difficult, nothing could prepare me for the sheer adrenaline of kicking doors down and crashing into unfamiliar households.

Chaplain Acheson used to say that fear gives birth to anger. After living in the vortex of uncertainty, the anxiety of approaching an unseen enemy behind every corner became excruciating. I started leaning heavily on Xanax to calm my nerves. I sought out a counselor the day after my bunkmate was shot in the head; I felt like I was ready to snap. Years later, in a counseling session, I would learn that fear and anger were very appropriate reactions to traumatic events, and not a sign of mental illness. According to the assigned mental health professionals on our base, the real cause of concern would be a soldier's inability to feel any anger. "The flat-lining of emotions is the first sign of sociopathic behavior," they said.

So I embraced my rage and squeezed the trigger every chance I got. It was like a codependency, an outlet for the chemicals in my brain to feel the euphoric rush of dopamine and endorphins unleashed from the prefrontal cortex through the limbic system and down my spinal cord. "Remember, these synthetic chemicals can become addictive," my counselor warned.

So I became a drug addict. The temporary satisfaction of a chemical release came from the spraying of an AR-15 into a dark room full of unknown statistics. I began to shiver at the thought of riding in a Hummer through the crowded streets with snipers on

38

every roof. One more Xanax, one more bullet. I became addicted to the adrenaline.

After six months of routine missions, I had grown weary of the monotony of front door crashing, ominous shouting, machine-gun leveraging, and pistol-whipping. I was becoming increasingly agitated at almost everyone within eyesight, including the men in my own unit. I wanted to go back to Charleston. I wanted to drink on the beach and surf at sunset, and my mind began to reminisce about the rickety old farmhouse and the stumbling through doors wide open into the waiting arms of Sierra and her promise to leave the light on.

All of a sudden, a bullet snapped above my head, slapping the exterior wall of the house we were about to invade. I ducked and ran for cover through the front door of the closest house on the city block. Our unit of seven men had been assigned the mission of searching the homes on this block, in pursuit of Al-Qaeda sympathizers, but we began to take fire from two snipers across the street. I'm not sure where the other men on my team dispersed to, but I clutched my helmet and began to scream into my radio for backup, then disappeared into the first house I could find. I heard shouting from across the street, and chaos ensuing.

Fortunately, the house that I had taken cover in had been abandoned. I peered out the window from behind a towel being used as a makeshift curtain, and I could see movement on the roof of the building across the street. I heard one of the men in my unit calling my name, and I shouted back to let him know where I was. Then I stood up, knocked out the glass window with the butt of my rifle, and began to spray bullets in the direction of the snipers across the way. I held down the trigger aggressively, pouring gunfire relentlessly toward the roof. The shell casings dropped at the floor beside me, and after thirty seconds (which seemed like an eternity), I laid back to wait for the reaction. All I heard was silence.

Eventually, I heard the sound of the front door opening down the hall and yelling, "Winter!" Never had I been so relieved to hear my name. One by one, the men of our unit assembled inside the doorway where I had taken cover. Additional reinforcements arrived on the scene as the radio operatives commanded assistance. We took an inventory of our losses, and came to the tragic realization that the enemy snipers had picked off two of our guys, including Eric Morrison, the driver of our Humvee. The second soldier killed was brand new to our unit, and I had never even met him. It was only his third day in Baghdad. I watched as the others hoisted Morrison off the ground and carry his lifeless body away, with his left arm missing. My eyes glazed over as I remembered a conversation I'd had with him just a few hours before he was killed. We had made plans to work out that night after dinner. Instead, I would spend the rest of the evening getting cozy with Absolut Vodka and a bottle of anti-anxiety medication.

They say you should never mix alcohol with prescription drugs, that it can mess with the chemicals in your brain, that combining the two can lead to dangerous consequences. But I was never good at chemistry, and mixed with a dose of apathy, I decided to roll the dice. How's this for a lethal combination: a disillusioned soldier who didn't even believe in the mission? A self-destructive prodigal who had no home to which he could return?

Signing up for the Armed Forces and willingly moving into a war zone was one of the greatest risks a human being can take, so the idea of "getting in trouble" for drinking alcohol on a mandatory dry base was not something that scared me. Before he died, Morrison showed me how to easily acquire alcohol; some of the men in our unit had it shipped in mouthwash containers, and the vodka was never intercepted. For the right price, you could satisfy almost every craving you itched for.

Fortunately, there were no assigned missions for the next two days, so I could sleep off the worst hangover of my life. I stayed in my bunk, listening to Zach de la Rocha as he raged against the machine. I did pushups and sit ups, and I drank some more. I reached for my old, tattered spiral-bound notebook and continued to scribble words to resemble a letter to my mother. It had taken me six months, and I had managed to squeeze out three sentences:

> Hey Mom, how are you? I'm fine. Well, not really. The truth is I'm really upset you didn't even come to see me off the day I left for a war I don't even believe in.

After a while, it dawned on me that although I could borrow some stamps from someone, I had nowhere to send the letter. By then, I didn't even know if my mother was still living at the same address. One of our last conversations included something about her finding an apartment to lease with her new husband. But I supposed that maybe some things are better left unsaid. My counselor briefly discussed the benefits of writing down my feelings in a journal every day, so I got a separate notebook for my personal thoughts.

> I don't want to live like this.

> Why can't I get it together?

> I don't like it here, but I don't like it there, either. I feel so alone, but I hate crowds. I want to believe in God, but I also want to believe in the pot of gold at the end of the rainbow and unicorns. But, you know, right now, just about the only thing I believe in is the power of a moment, when time just grinds to a halt and stands still. I believe in burning marshmallows and drinking Coronas on the beach with bare feet and shifting sand, and friends who love you unconditionally.

The next day was a bit of a blur as I returned to routine duties with the men in my unit. Although we didn't talk about the fatalities, it was clearly on everyone's minds. We discussed strategic efforts that might be more effective in the future, and were debriefed on proper radio communications. As it turns out, screaming profanities over the deafening roar of explosions are not easy to decipher from the command center. We spent the rest of the afternoon with further discussions about President Obama's plans to cut defense spending, and the implications of fewer troops in the Middle East My eyes began to glaze over after the second torturous hour of an irrelevant lecture from our commanding officer. He was a pompous jock with a loud mouth, and he was from Ohio, which pretty much meant he was born to lose at just about everything. I thought back to the time when Morrison once stole his Buckeyes cap and dropped it into the toilet of the Porta-John across the street. We all took turns leaving subtle messages for the "armpit of America," otherwise known as Ohio.

That evening at the dinner table, I overheard the Black Beret group talking about an event in which Cameron had participated. This highly trained crew of Special Forces operatives had recently been involved in a tactical mission involving the infiltration of an enemy base. According to the story, a row of single houses in a volatile neighborhood had been suspected to be a base of operation for some of Al-Qaeda's masterminds. Cam had been one of three soldiers assigned the duty of crashing through the back door, and providing cover for the other men coming through the front entrance. I listened to one of the witnesses retell the story: "Someone had detonated a smoke bomb, and they couldn't get a visual of anyone else in the room. Cam began to scream for everyone in the house to show their hands, and all he heard was the sound of a baby crying." Just then someone else cut into the conversation, adding, "Is it true that the Intel had been faulty? I mean, I heard the only people in the house were women and children." As the story continued, Cam had successfully deescalated the potentially violent situation by communicating to the rest of his unit that there were innocent civilians in the house. No shots were fired, and there were no casualties of war.

I left the dinner table and went to look for Cam at his bunk. His bed was made, but he was nowhere to be found. It seemed like every time I tried to catch up with him, he was off rescuing someone, fighting wartime evil with a Superman cape. Even his bunkmate said Cam was hardly ever around. I left another message for him to call me, and then I suddenly got the urge to call Sierra. It would have been very early in the morning in Charleston, but I took the risk and dialed her number anyway. After a few rings, she picked up.

"Good morning, Cam!" she answered. Considering the long-distance number calling in from Baghdad, she must have assumed that the call had been coming from him. My heart sank. "Sorry to disappoint you, Sierra. It's just me," I said, immediately regretting the decision to call. Now it was just awkward.

"Jordan? How are you? Is Cam okay?" Sierra asked, very logically and even more nervously. She had probably assumed that a random call at the crack of dawn could only mean bad news. "Cam's fine, Sierra," I said "I'm sorry to bother you so early. I've just been thinking about you a lot lately, and really missing Folly Beach. How are you doing? Tell me something good."

I waited for her to respond, hoping that she didn't take this phone call as some kind of forward or inappropriate gesture. She let out a sigh, and I could imagine her sitting up in her bed and looking out the windows.

"Something good?" she echoed. "Well, the sun is just starting to rise over the Atlantic Ocean right now. How's that for good?" I suddenly remembered all the times we had stayed up all night with beach parties and bonfires and surfing, and those precious memories brought a smile to my face. It had been a long time since I had smiled.

I told Sierra all about Cameron's adventures, including his heroic efforts to defuse a bomb threat in a parked car, as well as the most recent incident involving a house full of women and children who could have easily been hurt or killed. It did not surprise me that Cam had never mentioned any of these exploits to Sierra— he rarely talked about himself. She was very curious about his disposition, and was counting down the days until we could return for an extended leave.

Of course, Sierra couldn't let the conversation get too far without her trademark question: "And where have you been, Jordan?" I shuffled my feet as the question brought back so many memories of inebriated guilt. "I've been up to no good," I responded dutifully. I told her I had been growing anxious and frustrated with our combat missions, that I just wanted to go home and return to my job at the lumberyard. We talked about her job and working with children on the autism spectrum. She told me that every night, she sits on her porch, has a cup of tea as she prays for her boys to return, and whispers, "I'll leave the light on for you."

By the time I hung up the phone, I felt a thousand times better. It felt good to be known and loved by true friends, and to be reminded of tenderness in a world of violence. Whenever I was losing hope in humanity, I could think of Sierra sitting on her porch with a cup of tea and her signature red toenails polished with 50 shades of innocence.

Chapter 5

The Least of These

Two weeks had passed since I'd last seen Cam. When all else failed, I always knew that I could catch him at the midweek chapel service. But Chaplain Acheson said he hadn't seen Cameron in while. I was deeply distracted by his abrupt absence, and I had a difficult time hearing anything taught or discussed during the Bible Study. My mind was a million miles away, and I realized that I had probably showed up for the wrong reasons, and now that I thought about it, the free coffee was too weak.

After a routine assignment to patrol the neighboring blocks, I returned to the base and once again tried to call Cam. There was still no answer again, and I decided that I was going to track him down. I found a few guys from the Black Beret unit and they each had different accounts of his latest sightings. Finally, an acquaintance overheard my question and asked me, "Did you check the field behind the hospital? I think he's been hanging out over there in the evenings."

The field behind the hospital, I knew, was an area of popular destination for many of the local children who congregated there after evening prayers. Perhaps it was an outworking of his faith why Cam wanted to be there, or maybe he was just trying to offset some of his own guilt. It was a short walk to the field, just down a few side streets. By now, the sun was beginning to set beneath a purple sky, and the desert heat began to be chased away by the evening breeze.

Directly behind the brick wall surrounding the hospital was a plot of land swimming with Iraqi children chasing around a deflated soccer ball. The frequent gusts of wind had created clouds of dust trampled beneath the bare feet of several dozen boys, and a few courageous little girls as well. There were no nets or official goalposts, just a few jackets strewn about as field markers to identify where the boundaries existed.

The irony was not lost on me. When it comes to laughter and competition and courage, boundaries are about as irrelevant as a tattered jacket in a field of dirt. We have our ideologies and our concrete assumptions about good and evil. We like our brick walls around hospitals and our machine guns to defend our borders. But some things transcend boundaries, and the authenticity of an honest scoreboard is enough motivation to make children lose their ever-loving minds over a backyard ball game.

And sure enough, there was Cameron, in the middle of the pile of dust. He was the appointed goalie of the losing team, and was diving in the dirt to save loose balls from passing through his invisible fortress. He was shouting and laughing and I could hear him giving instructions to his young teammates. I watched from a distance as he dished out high-fives, and I could tell that these young boys and girls were fascinated with him. I found out later that many of these street kids had become orphans in a war they didn't fully understand. They adored Cam because he was older, like a big brother or father, and they were starved for attention. Some of them had lost their fathers to the various fractions of Islamic extremism, and the imminent fate of almost every kid on that field would include their own dates with a holy war that would consume and forever change them. But in the twilight, one thing mattered... chasing that saggy ball with a reckless abandon.

Eventually Cam saw me sitting on the sidelines, and excused

himself from the game. While the children continued on in his absence, he came over to sit down next to me. "Hey, man, what's up?" he asked, wiping his brow from the beads of sweat falling relentlessly from his brow. I offered him what was left of my bottle of water and replied, "Well, I haven't seen you in a while, and I've been looking for you everywhere," I responded. "Somebody said you were out here for some reason. So I came out to see what you've been up to..." My voice trailed off as he finished off the rest of the water, pouring the last few drops over his head. He was still breathing heavy, but he motioned over to the children to let them know he was heading back to the base. "I've been hanging out with my new friends," he said, smiling as he watched them for another minute, engrossed in their game and squealing in glee.

While we began to walk slowly back to our base, we talked about the psychological toll that war can take on a man. Cameron confessed he was having a really difficult time sleeping at night, knowing that he was responsible for making orphans out of the same children he had befriended. He understood the complexities of war, but the faces of innocent boys and girls seemed to weigh heavy on his conscience. I've been thinking...what if Jesus actually meant that stuff about loving our enemies?" Cam said. I didn't offer a response, so he continued. "What would it look like to reach out to the most vulnerable of children and try to win their hearts so that someday they don't grow up to become enemies?"

We stood outside under the lights at the gate of our base, and talked for hours. Cam poured his heart out, not holding anything back. He was growing disillusioned with the culture of violence and the physical and emotional weight of a machine gun in his hands. He had come here to serve his country with pride, but as time marched on, he had grown disinterested in political ideologies. The sleepless nights and violent days had taken a toll on his otherwise sunny disposition. I could see it in his eyes, and he was growing weary. One thing was certain: We both missed South Carolina, and couldn't wait to get home.

Homecoming King

It would be another three months of active combat duty before we were granted a leave of absence. The leave couldn't have come at a better time, as July was approaching, and we would be able to spend Independence Day with our loved ones in Charleston, with a scheduled return the second week of August. And by the time we boarded the flight home, I had mentally begun to check out. All I could think about was home.

The violent insanity of Bagdad in those months absorbed some of the highest-calculated totals of American soldiers killed or injured in active combat. And as the war on terror spread toward Afghanistan, the war within my heart was also being waged. It had been so long since I cared about anything, the casualties of war seemed to have no effect on me.

As for Cam, he continued to wrestle through the political theories and his faith convictions. If he wasn't playing soccer with the local children, you could often find him lingering to talk with Chaplain Acheson. Cam would ask difficult questions with rapid fire until the Army Chaplain would interrupt him with a request for "one question at a time, please."

At our layover in the airport, I asked Cam if he had any regrets about his voluntary enlistments. "The only thing I regret is having not already proposed to Sierra. It's a wonder she's waited for me this long," Cam said. He checked the flight number of our plane, and continued his thought. "The more violence, greed, and corruption I see in this world, the more love I have for her." I sat down next to him and looked at him while he scrolled through the pictures on his cell phone. It seemed like his love for her was the medicine that kept his heart strong.

My heart, however, seemed beyond repair. The carnage that had accumulated from all the battles, and the stories of shock and awe over the past several months, had added fuel to my fire. It was like I had finally found an outlet for all of the anger and depression of my adolescence—there was nothing an automatic rifle couldn't remedy. My propensity to seek comfort through the familiar acceptance and warmth of hard liquor had also become a coping mechanism in a world at war.

Once we boarded the aircraft, Cam scrambled to rearrange the seating so that we could sit next to each other. An elderly man in a Florida Marlins jacket gladly volunteered to give up his seat for our accommodations. Cam buckled his seat belt and reached for a sports magazine. I held a bookmark from the pages of Tolstoy's *War and Peace*, but my mind drifted. Although he never talked about his knee injury, I knew Cam still harbored a wounded heart from the loss of his athletic scholarship. I wondered about his plans after our enlistment.

"Are you still interested in finishing college, or a career in Public Administration?" I asked. He didn't look up at me, just flipped through the pages in his magazine before answering. "Honestly, man, after all this, the only thing I want to do is make it back to Sierra, and maybe marry her and start a family. I don't care if I have to work at Taco Bell or back at the community pool again, as long as I'm back in my hometown with the people I love."

It would make sense for him to have such an affinity to his land, and these people. His roots grew deep in the South Carolina soil, and his family was widely respected throughout the community. The greatest evidence of this reality would happen several hours later, when our plane touched down in our hometown.

As we exited the plane, a small crowd of friends and family had been waiting to greet us (and by "us," I mean Cameron). There were Welcome Home signs, flags, and cheers as we hurried toward our supporters, where Cam was first greeted by his mother, who held him tightly and unleashed a fountain of joyful tears. His father was there too, with a visible pride in his eyes as he hugged Cam and clutched at his shirt. There were a few dozen other familiar faces that were gracious in their greeting to me as well, although I hardly knew them. They respected the service of our duty, and were vocal in their honor and appreciation of our status. I spotted Mrs. Norman, the guidance counselor at my high school, and gave her a hug. I'd always liked her. She had always advised me to consider the Armed Forces as a means to pay for my college tuition someday.

While I was talking with her, my eyes scanned the crowd for Sierra. The chaos of the crowd had made it difficult for me to see Cameron, but from across the room, I saw him reach out for her as she approached him. Sierra squealed with joy as she literally jumped into his arms. He lifted her up, and I could tell by the way his shoulders were shaking that he was crying heavily. Everyone and everything around them disappeared, and their embrace reminded me of their first dance in tenth grade, when he first declared his love for her.

That night, we had an epic reunion at Sierra's house. Almost a year had passed since we had all been together, and the war had a way of dividing life up into two halves: the innocence of childhood, and the brokenness of adulthood. The laughter and games and the inside jokes and beach parties all seemed like a different lifetime, and the white noise of exploding bombs had a way of deafening the voices of yesterday.

By the time I had arrived to Sierra's old farmhouse, I had already had too much to drink. I had stopped by my local watering hole, The Alibi, on the way, and I saw a couple of guys I used to shoot pool with. They seemed legitimately glad to see me, and Angie bought me some drinks on the house. Considering I had no bloodline or family to receive me, the bar crowd seemed like my only alternative. I regretted the fact that I had never sent the letter to my mother, and I contemplated stopping by Aunt Tracy's to see her. Nevertheless, I angled the pool stick toward the 8-ball and remained detached from familial responsibility.

Sierra's street was jam-packed with parked cars. I walked up the driveway toward her front porch, spotting an American flag through the darkness. A bright light illuminated the rest of the driveway, and having had *maybe* had one drink too many, I stumbled up the steps. I could hear laughter and music drifting inside, and I reached for the doorknob. Before I could turn it, Sierra opened the door to greet me. She stood there in a yellow sundress (barefoot, of course). I looked at her bare feet, bronzed from the unfiltered Carolina sunshine. Instead of her typical red nail polish, her toes were painted yellow to match her dress. She put her hands on her hips, grinned and let out a false sigh and said, "Jordan, where have you been?"

It was the most sentimental greeting I ever could have asked for, a beautiful moment, and I collected it for a deposit into my memory bank for years to come. My routine answer was the same as it had always been: "I've been up to no good, Sierra."

She nodded with a smile. "Well, I forgive you. How about you come on in here and sit down? We're all fixin' to eat. Are you hungry?"

Although Cameron and I had both changed dramatically and permanently since our departure for Iraq, Sierra had remained the same. She scurried around the house, playing the perfect hostess, making sure everyone had a drink in their hand or food on their plate. She took time to speak personally with everyone in the room, and wouldn't dare let anyone help her clean up. As the guests finally began to clear out, only a handful of friends remained seated at the table.

Sierra's friend Cassie had recently moved away for college but was home for summer vacation. After a while, it became fairly clear that Sierra was trying to set us up. When Cassie stepped outside to receive a phone call from her friend, Sierra whispered, "What do you think of her?" I looked toward the front door through which Cassie had disappeared. "She's nice, I guess. Why do you ask?" Sierra brushed her hair back behind her ear and said, "Well, I know she's really into you!"

Just then, Cassie returned, apologizing for the sudden interruption. I'd had too many drinks to make clear sense of that brief transaction, so I kept my mouth shut. While we sat outside on the front porch talking, Cassie told me all about her college courses, and her hopes to someday become an interior designer. I vaguely recall having met her once before that night, but I must have been too drunk at the time to remember our conversation then too.

Cam and Sierra joined us out on the porch, and Cam and I shared some of our experiences in Baghdad. Sierra seemed less interested in the stories of combat and much more curious about the psychological toll that the war had been taking on us. While Cameron shared his frustrations, Cassie huddled close to me, and inadvertently touched my thigh with her hand while she was talking with Sierra. I looked down at her hand on my thigh, and then up at Sierra, who had noticed it as well. She winked at me, and then I realized what was happening: Cassie had been invited over for many reasons, not the least of which was meeting me.

As the evening crept later and later into the night, my head began to throb from the fullness of the day. I had looked at my watch and realized that it had not yet been synchronized with Eastern Standard Time, and neither had I. My whole rhythm of sleep and consciousness had become confused, but I was exhausted. "It's getting late, and I need to get on home," I said. But as I stood up to leave, my head began to spin and I had to sit back down for a minute.

"Jordan, don't be ridiculous! You've had too much to drink and I have plenty of room. How 'bout y'all crash here? I've got a couch and an extra bedroom!" Sierra helped me to my feet. Cam seemed to agree that under the circumstances, he could sleep in the king-sized bed in the guest bedroom. Cassie had already arranged with Sierra to spend the night as well, so the four of us would be crashing under the same roof.

As soon as I lowered my body onto the couch, I collapsed into a deep sleep. I don't remember anything else about the evening, but when I woke up in the morning, Cassie was sleeping on the couch next to me. I knew that nothing had happened between us physically, but it was nice to feel the pulse of a woman beside me. A blue comforter was wrapped around her shoulders, and her blonde hair was tucked back behind her ears. I tried to remember the details of the conversation the night before, but I could only remember the touch and the wink and the overall awkwardness of being set up. I could only imagine how Cam and Sierra must have described me to her, and if I had known about this little matchmaking scheme ahead of time, I would have worn my lucky jeans. I never lose when I am wearing them, and with all of my zero experience with the ladies, I needed all the help I could get.

It was early in the morning, and everyone else in the house was still asleep. I slowly eased myself up from the couch, trying not to wake up Cassie. As I stood up and began to stretch, she yawned and fluttered her eyes open. We looked at each other in the dimness of the morning light, but did not speak. I smiled at her and she smiled back, and I slowly walked out the front door. The front porch light had been left on throughout the night. Sierra would have it no other way.

Homecoming Queen

I spent the next two weeks trying to rebuild a relationship with my mother. Despite several attempts to contact her, I had very little success. Although I received a voicemail from her once, the rest of my phone calls to the number she gave went unanswered. Finally, I tracked down her address from my Aunt Tracy, and I set out to visit her. As it turned out, my mom had been through her second divorce, citing irreconcilable differences, and it sent her into a tailspin of depression. She had been working through a temp agency, but lost her job after calling in sick too often. Aunt Tracy told me she was living with some guy named Ron in a trailer park, about 15 minutes from the county line.

I drove out to the trailer park, trying to remember the last time I had even seen her, and I shuddered when I realized it'd been at least three years. Our last conversation included a casual goodbye and something about her going on vacation with a friend. It seemed that all of the anger I had toward my father had been redirected toward my mom.

When I knocked on the door, there was no answer. I strained my ear to the door to listen, but all I could hear was the sound of a bird chirping and the rustling of the summer leaves in the trees above the mobile home. Just as I turned to leave, the door opened. A man stood in the doorway, but he did not speak. He was wearing blue jeans and sported a red bandana over his unkempt hair. His t-shirt had yellow armpit stains, which he clearly knew and did not care. As if the scene could get any more cliché, a cigar dangled from his lips, shielding his excessive overbite. I could practically hear banjo music playing and pigs squealing in the distance. "I'm looking for Pamela Winter," I said. The silence was incredibly awkward as the man in the doorway, continuing to say nothing, just boring holes into my face. "Is this the right address?" I asked. "I'm her son, Jordan."

After what seemed like an eternity, he turned to his side and called out to my mother. He mumbled behind his unlit cigar, "You ain't never told me you had a son." In that moment, a piece of me died. I didn't know if I wanted to laugh or cry. I felt the temptation to throat punch this hillbilly and make him eat his expired cigar. I wanted to burn the decrepit mobile home to the ground, and rescue my mother from the fangs of hopelessness. *How could someone become so lost in the oblivion of indifference?*

Indifference seemed to be in my bloodstream, however. As much as I wondered about my mother's downward spiral, I could feel those same feelings of indifference unraveling in my own heart. I had stopped caring about most things several years earlier, and as I waited for my mother to come to the door, I felt the invading grip of hopelessness.

The door opened wider, and a woman slowly emerged from the shadows. It took me a few seconds to recognize her as my mom. She had aged significantly and practically looked like a ghost. My childhood memories pictured her frozen in a beautiful portrait with long, dark hair, shining eyes, her dazzling (if infrequent) smile. She'd been so pretty, despite the neglect. And even though I didn't like her, I loved her.

"Jordan!" She cried enthusiastically. "Look at you!" My mother walked down the steps to greet me, and as she got closer, I held out my arms to hug her. In the brightness of the sun, I could see the bruises on her face. Her dress was tattered, her lips cracked, parched, dry. As I held her, I felt her frailty. My mother had been so beaten down over the years from life that she had lost herself completely. All of my angst toward her negligence was absorbed in a bleeding heart of mercy, and I realized in that moment, she didn't just fail to protect me… I had also failed to protect her. What had taken me so long to contact her and make sure she was okay? To tell her I loved her?

I told her all about my experiences in Baghdad, and that I was fighting on the front lines. I told her stories of heroism and danger. I explained that I'd been granted a leave of absence, and while I was home I wanted to find her, and tell her I loved her and forgave her. She let out a huge sob, and I realized my mom had become the shell of a woman who had emotionally flat-lined. As she trembled in my arms, I looked back at the man in the doorway. He stood with his hands on his hips, as if to supervise. I whispered, "Mom, where are these bruises from? Tell me the truth."

She didn't answer, but instead shook her head and continued to cling to me. By now, my eyes were locked on the violent abuser that had held her captive. "Go get in the truck, Mom," I said, very quietly. "I need to introduce myself properly to this guy." My mother didn't say a word, but her silence seemed to approve of what she rightfully assumed was about to happen. I walked her to the Jeep and opened the passenger door, held it for her, and said, "Just sit tight, Mom. I'll be right back."

I turned back to walk up the driveway toward the mobile home, where the man had not moved or even flinched from his stance. As I inched toward him, I asked, "Are you right-handed or left?" He didn't move, but shouted back, "What are you talkin' 'bout, boy?"

I took three more strides up the stairs and seized him by the throat. His cigar fell down the inside of his shirt, and his eyes nearly popped out of his head. I continued to choke him until he collapsed to the ground. I assumed he was right-handed, so I wrenched his hand back and squeezed it until I heard his wrist crack. He would never lift his hand toward my mother ever, ever again.

"Let me explain something to you. My mother has been beaten and kicked around her whole life. She's done absolutely nothing to deserve it! Nothing!" I screamed in his ear, shaking with rage. Instead of killing the man with my bare fists, I opted instead to slap him three times (once for each year that I had not heard from my mother). I stood tall and turned to leave, vowing to kill him if he ever tried to hurt her again.

I walked back to my Jeep and climbed in the driver's seat. My mom was looking the other way, out the window. She wasn't crying anymore, but she wasn't happy either. I put the gear in reverse and took the rural route back home. We drove in silence, save the hum of the engine on the open road. I wondered if war had changed me, or exposed me, or maybe a bit of both. The ancient debate—nature versus nurture—continued within me. My own journey toward self-discovery was just being initiated.

'Til Death Do Us Part

I brought my mother back to live in my apartment, and I set her up with everything she would need to reach her independence. Aunt Tracy agreed to take her shopping for new clothes, and I paid the next six months of rent in advance from my savings account. We created a joint bank account, and each month, I received a direct deposit from the United States Army. The utilities remained in my name, and my military paycheck would provide for her needs.

The remaining days of my vacation leave were filled with meaningful conversations with my mother. We talked about the war, and plans for the future. We talked about everything under the sun, except my father. That would remain an unwritten chapter, and I was not ready to open that book.

On the evening before our scheduled return to Baghdad, Cameron called me and said he wanted me to meet him at the beach, that it was important. Whenever we referred to "the beach," there was always an assumed exact location of our meeting: Sugar Beach, which was a surf break about a mile from the state park. I hung up the phone and threw on my favorite sweatshirt. Despite its notorious heat, the beaches of South Carolina can get quite a chill off the ocean, especially after sunset.

I drove out to the beach, spotted Cam's car, and parked my Jeep next to it. As I squinted eastward toward the shoreline, I could see someone standing near the water in a distance. As I walked closer, I realized that the blurry image had come into focus, turning into two images. Cameron held Sierra in a familiar embrace, and my eyes could not differentiate where he stopped and she started. They must have seen me coming from the headlights of my car, because in the fading daylight, Sierra waved with both arms. Even without electricity, she always left the light on for me.

As I approached them, Cameron turned to face me. "Hey, bro. Thanks for meeting us down here on such short notice." In the moonlit reflection off the water, I could see he looked serious, but very happy. Sierra couldn't stop grinning either, and I knew that whatever they had to share was of utmost importance. I greeted them with a hug, both arms wrapped around my two best friends.

"What's going on?" I asked. Before anything more could be said, Sierra motioned for me to shush. As she pressed her finger dramatically to her lips, I realized why she had intentionally chosen her left ring finger. A diamond sparkled in the moonlight, and she grinned from ear to ear. Nobody said anything for a minute, and in the silence, I could hear the sound of waves crashing into the shoreline beyond us.

"You proposed! When? How? Why didn't you tell anyone?" I asked. Cam laughed and nodded, having presumably anticipated the barrage of questions. "I know," he said. "Let me explain…" It wasn't just a proposition; it was a covenant of marriage.

The three of us plopped down in the sand, and Cameron began to share the series of events. As he began to tell me the details, Sierra occasionally interrupted to clarify or contribute additional detail to the unfolding narrative. As it had turned out, Sierra had been struggling to keep up with the utility payments for her inherited farmhouse. Her hours had been cut even more at work, and while we had been in Baghdad, she'd been barely hanging on financially.

And for the past several months, Cameron had been saving for a diamond ring to give Sierra. Without telling a soul, he had been planning on proposing during this extended leave. But earlier this morning as they walked the beach, Cameron simply said,

"What are we waiting for? Let's get married today!" Sierra had no objection, and agreed: they were on fire with an urgent love, and did not want to wait another year for his next scheduled vacation home.

So they called for their pastor, Ryan Blevins, and invited only Cameron's parents to witness their marital vows. This was by their choice, a very private setting. Sierra had no family for which to observe her blowing out of the candles. And yet in a way, by coming from nowhere, Sierra could claim to have come from everywhere. Sierra's lack of witnesses meant she could inherit the observation of having everyone. Years later, Sierra would remember the sun and the moon and the stars as the faithful witnesses in the sky to the covenant established between her and Cameron.

"We've talked about this for a few years. It wasn't a matter of 'if,' it was always a matter of 'when,'" Cameron said. "From now on, Sierra will receive a direct deposit of my military pay, and she'll be able to afford the cost of home repair and renovations. She is my home."

They seemed to live at the intersection between chivalry and practicality. But at the core of their love for each other was a profound selflessness that seemed to dissolve into the needs of the other. Sierra had always sat on the sidelines during Cameron's football games, cheering her heart out for her home team and her all-star player, but in the same fashion, Cam had always been Sierra's biggest fan too. He absolutely adored her, and would do anything humanly possible to make sure she was encouraged, celebrated, memorized, and adored.

In many ways, I was jealous of their love for each other. Having never experienced the sharing of selflessness in a committed relationship, theirs was the only representation that I had known to last. My own parents had contributed to the indifference and bitterness of broken promises, and I had grown jaded over the years. But here, in the shimmering reflection of the moon off the rolling waves, I felt the presence of true love.

Chapter 6

Greater Love Hath No Man

The harsh return to the chaotic blur of smoke and blood was a stark contrast from the warm embrace of Sierra's front porch. Within a few minutes of our airplane landing, I was jolted back to the reality that evil exists in the form of greed, oil, and terror, and I was assigned the duty to represent a nation born in the furnace of hope. As if it were possible, insidious attacks had actually escalated to an all-time high. Fatalities increased, injuries skyrocketed, and suicide bombings continued to complicate an already confusing war. How do you fight a man you cannot see, a coward hiding in a crowd of innocent people? And at what point do ethics and honor get pushed away behind a happy trigger and a migraine headache? It seemed like there were reports of Jihad bombings in crowded marketplaces daily. Although the Al-Qaeda virus had seemed to dissipate to the mountainous terrain of Afghanistan, the citizens of Baghdad continued to live in a polarizing nightmare of confusion. Sticks and stones divided families, while children walked around in the fog, the innocent bystanders of an ancient hate.

The day after our return to active combat, I found myself leaning more heavily into the coping mechanism of painkillers and anxiety medication. They say you should never mix alcohol with prescription medications, but they also say you shouldn't mix politics with religion, but all religion is political, and all politics are religious, and therefore, in my mind, every drop of alcohol is nothing more than a liquid painkiller.

I became more of a recluse. As if I could become any more antisocial, the voluntary isolation allowed for me to escape the court of public opinion. And in the furnace of anxiety, my addictions developed a wide-rooted system of imbalance. I was fueled by the adrenaline of buildings on fire, and I lived explosions and the sound of shell casings dropping from an AR-15. It got to the point where I would get the shakes if I didn't add vodka to my Coke or clutch a cigarette in my hand. I preferred to sit alone on my bunk and put on headphones, listening to Rage Against the Machine until I fell asleep.

One of the guys in my unit worked as a medic, and he enabled my addiction. Not that I blamed him, but he made prescription painkillers readily available for the right price. I spent an absurd amount of time and money getting wasted in my room. At one point, my commanding officer noticed my growing detachment from daily assignments, and he forced me to work in the office for a week. Under the control of his constant supervision, I ached more than ever for the release of chemical assistance. He knew it, but I wasn't alone in this condition. There were several guys in our unit who had been finding unhealthy ways to cope with the stress of active combat. Somehow we were expected to clock in and out of a normal day, and dismiss the reality of our mission. It wasn't uncommon for men to work out in the gym for hours after a full workday, or overeat in the cafeteria from the stress of our assignment. Some of the men (and women) in our unit were increasingly agitated, fighting over card games or elbow room at the dinner table.

Every now and then, we were granted up to three days off in a row. The provision of ample time allowed for the days and weeks to pass more quickly. As I had learned back home in the county jail, time passes more quickly when you're asleep. When I reached my bunk, I turned off my cell phone and silenced the noise with earplugs. My eyes closed as I swallowed my Xanax with a shot of vodka, chased with more pills, and before too long my conscience was covered by a blanket of naked depression.

Later, I felt someone yanking on my foot, and awoke quickly from the kind of drowsy sleep where you wake up confused. I sat up immediately, and squinted as my eyes adjusted to the daylight. I didn't know what day or time it was. I didn't even know where I was. Once my eyes adjusted, I saw my best friend standing at the foot of my bunk.

Cameron stared at me for a few seconds, as I mumbled under my breath. He ignored my dismissive grunts. "Get dressed," he said. "You're coming with me."

I had no idea where he thought he was taking me, but I was *not* interested. I wanted to crawl under my blankets and stay there. He reached over and yanked the foam earplugs out of my ears. "Either get up yourself or I'll carry you," he said. I squinted through the glaring sunlight and could see he was angry. "What are you talking about?" I asked.

"You're in too deep this time," Cam said. He sat down on my bed, forcing me to sit up. "We need to talk. And if you don't want to talk to me, that's fine. But you're going to talk to someone." He tossed me a faded t-shirt as I reluctantly put on my shorts. He glanced over at my weapons, "Alcohol and prescription pills do not belong in the same room as an AR-15 assault rifle and a psychologically unstable soldier."

An hour later, I was sitting inside the office of the resident psychiatrist on our base. He was paid handsomely well to diagnose symptoms of struggling or depressed soldiers and propose an effective treatment plan. I'd seen this movie before. It all reminded me of the movie *A Few Good Men* ("You can't handle the truth!"). He waited for me to open up and explain my recent spiral into addiction and depression. Meanwhile, Cameron waited outside the office, seated in the waiting room.

"Tell me about when you stopped caring," the doctor said. I stared up at his degrees on the wall, one from Northwestern University, and another from Stanford. Clearly this doctor had seen and heard it all. "What was your name again?" I asked. Without waiting for him to respond, I squinted over at one of his degrees. "Pavlock. Dr. Pavlock, I don't know when I stopped caring. Probably the day my dad went to prison for killing two kids. Or maybe it was the day my mom emotionally ran off, leaving me to raise myself. Or maybe it when the assistant principal suspended me for one too many absences, because he didn't realize that I had to work on Tuesday and Thursday mornings in order to pay the electric bill." I continued to vent. "Then I come over here and get paid to kill people. Do you know what kind of psychological damage that does to a man? Last week I emptied a clip of bullets into a building without clarity as to whom exactly I was shooting at. All I know is that we were under attack, and I don't even know who the enemy is!"

It felt so good to rant, to finally let it all out. I stood up and paced around and opened up about my borderline sociopathic indifference. Although I had not been officially diagnosed, it certainly felt like I was living in the two extreme polarities of energy and sadness. I told him about not getting one single vote for student council in tenth grade, and how I had grown to become invisible over the years. He furiously scribbled notes, trying to keep up with me.

"Jordan, have you ever heard of the fugue state?" He asked quietly. I had no idea what he had said because I was craving for a cigarette, or a bottle, or a gun. He motioned for me to sit back down.

"Do you ever feel detached from reality?" he probed. "Not like insanity, but it's more like a temporary state of disassociation...

a dreamlike state." He went on to describe a relatively new psychological phenomena: a diagnosis of mental and emotional detachment from pain, but separating feelings and emotions from certain events. "This is not a prolonged mental absence," he said. "It is fleeting. One might feel as if he were hovering over his body watching his life unfold like scenes in a movie."

I looked at him, unsure as to whether he was crazy, brilliant, or just a mind reader. But the truth is, I had felt those moments of temporary disassociation, perhaps just suppressing the reality of the evil to which I was contributing. "Yeah," I admitted. "I do feel that way sometimes. Like it's all a dream I can't wake up from. I find myself mentally checking out in the middle of a conversation, and sometimes even in the middle of an assigned mission."

Dr. Pavlock continued to ask me more about the nature of my addictions and the amount of my alcohol consumption. I purposefully did not tell him about the abuse of prescription medication because I didn't trust his confidentiality. Instead, I held back, and suppressed the depth of my depravity. After 50 minutes, he stood to his feet and shook my hand. "Thank you for coming to see me today, Jordan. And you should also thank your friend Cameron who arranged for this intervention."

I opened the door and found Cam waiting patiently in the other room. He didn't look agitated or impatient, just concerned. I agreed to meet with Dr. Pavlock again, setting up weekly appointments as needed. Cameron stood as I approached him, and together we walked outside.

"We don't have to talk about it today," he said. "But I want you to know eventually we're going to have to confront this demon and set it free." The beauty of Cameron's friendship was revealed when he intentionally used the word 'we' in the description of my growing addiction. He seemed to enter into my brokenness and helped to engage the darkness. I didn't know how to thank him fully, so I detached myself from the discomfort and allowed my mind to hover over the awkwardness of the conversation, sort of like that fugue state Dr. Pavlock had described.

We walked back to the cafeteria for a cup of coffee. All around us, our unit men were warmly greeting Cameron. It brought back memories of high school—whenever Cam walked into the room, everyone called his name and ignored me. He had continued to garner respect by the way he treated others with kindness, and always seemed to remember everyone's name (unlike me; I have always been horrible at remembering peoples' names). Cam could walk into a crowded room and win each person over individually by offering the gift of his undivided attention. He was never in a hurry. He never looked past someone to the next person to talk to. He was centered and fully present.

Cameron sat in the corner, away from the noise of the rowdy soldiers, and motioned for me to take the seat across from him. When I sat down, he began to bless our food with a sacramental prayer. He thanked God for the blessing of this day, and the privilege of my friendship. He asked for strength and courage for tomorrow, and a routine list of other blessings. I just stared down at my plate, half-listening, waiting for his prayer to finish. But then he added a sentence that almost slipped right past me. "…And thank you, God, for the gift of Sierra and the delicate life growing inside her right now."

It took a second for the words to register, but when my cognitive delays caught up to the corresponding amen, I looked up at Cam, who was grinning ear to ear. "Yes, it's true," he said. "I got a letter from Sierra this morning!" He pulled out a folded envelope from his back pocket and slid it over to me. Inside the opened envelope were a brief letter and a picture "You are my sunshine, my only sunshine. You make me happy when skies are gray…" But the picture spoke a thousand words. Sierra was standing in front of her old farmhouse with a silhouette shadow beside her. In the picture, her hair was blowing in the wind, and her red sundress was clinging to her curves. In her right hand, she was holding a sign that simply read, "Hello, Daddy!" with her left hand placed over her stomach.

I immediately began to cry.

I don't know why I started to cry. Maybe it was the contrast of a world at war and the world we left behind, or was the depression of my own disillusionment and the brokenness of my own soul, colliding with the delicate innocence of this picture. Maybe I just missed Sierra. Maybe I was jealous. Maybe.

But my tears were also tears of joy. I was truly happy for my best friend, and as I stood to hug him, he just laughed without saying a word. Nothing really needed to be said. He was going to be an amazing father, and I could only hope to someday demonstrate the same kind of selflessness that he expressed to everyone every day. I sat back down and looked at the picture again. "I'm so happy for you, brother. I really am!" He just looked at me and nodded, and then he confessed, "To be honest, Jordan, I'm terrified! I'm overwhelmed with the possibilities and the hopes of giving our baby the best possible life imaginable." He went on to articulate his desire to have a large family, and a houseful of children running around that rickety old farmhouse firmly settled in the serene landscape of Charleston.

That evening, I returned to my room and rummaged through some old boxes until I found my journal. It had been a while since I wrote anything, but I was feeling inspired. After thumbing through the old entries, I scribbled a prayer.

Dear God:

If you really exist, I want to see you.

I had no idea that God would reveal Himself to me in the days and months ahead, but I could have never guessed that it would be in such a graphic expression of flesh and blood. Because at the time of that journal entry, my faith had hit an all-time low, and rock bottom seemed to have a hole in the basement floor.

If there were prescription pills anywhere to be found in Baghdad, I would hunt them down. Although it felt good to talk with Dr. Pavlock, it didn't solve the problem of my growing addiction to the chemical escape that calmed my nerves and helped me sleep. I began to pursue the coping mechanism of anxiety medication with a reckless abandon. If I was not actively involved in a combat mission, I was getting high or sleeping. I worked hard to build trust with a couple of other guys who also sought the remedy of self-medication. We exchanged prescription pills for every occasion. I had a remedy for both anxiety and depression. And if I couldn't sleep, there were pills for that too. If I needed more energy, there was a red pill, or a blue pill, until the ominous volume of a world at war was silenced in my head. Cameron was not oblivious to my choices, but we never talked about the areas of my hidden propensities.

Even though I'd agreed to weekly appointments with Dr. Pavlock, I stopped seeing him after just four sessions. I figured I would talk when I was ready to talk, but I wouldn't voluntarily spread out on his couch while he psychoanalyzed me. I didn't dislike him personally, but I didn't trust him. So I kept to myself, and I locked the world away.

The Order of Chaos

Six months had passed since my sessions with Dr. Pavlock. The 'fugue state' seemed to have become a permanent reality to my otherwise unbelievable world. I detached myself from emotion, separating myself from the reality that I had become very good at isolation and self-destruction. I was sincerely and purely motivated by the adrenaline that accompanied violence. I openly welcomed conflict, mouthed off at superior officers, and leaned into active combat.

One evening, I took a combination of pills, one for each of the runaway chemicals in my brain. I imagined that if I put all of the colorful pills into a blender, it would spit out a smoothie of infinite utopia. I locked the door, lowered the shades, and fell into a deep sleep.

Six hours later, I was awakened by the jolting blare of a siren sounding throughout the base. This emergency call was self-explanatory, and there wasn't a snooze button for this occasion. As a soldier, I had to respond to the call of duty. I rolled out of bed and put on my gear, not even stopping to brush my teeth or tie my shoes. I rushed to get fully dressed and ran down the hallway to report for action. The sound of the siren pounded in my head as it throbbed from the confusing signals sent from the chemicals in my brain.

As a growing number of soldiers gathered at the center of base, it appeared that nobody knew what was going on. Some of the guys were still bleary-eyed and still half-asleep, while others were still frantically buttoning their shirts. My eyes were glazed over from the chemical confusion of internal brain activity, and I wondered if this were the nirvana of the fugue state. *Was this a dream?*

We stood at attention as our commanding officer shouted information, including military instructions for the situation at hand. Our intelligence agencies had an urgent revelation, and Special Forces had pinpointed the exact location of several high-value targets of the Al-Qaeda web of terror. We were being advised of the location and would be sent out to bring them to justice, dead or alive.

It all happened so fast. Information was being spit out at an alarming rate of speed, and I still didn't even know if I was awake or sleeping. Within thirty minutes, I was dispatched with a convoy of four other units toward a warehouse on the north side of Bagdad. It had long since been a location of terrorist activity, but the early morning would be our time of exact offense. Quick Reaction Forces remained on standby as we received further instructions of engagement.

Adrenaline chased the chemicals in my bloodstream, my heart was pounding with fear and thrill, and my fingers felt numb. Even as I held my assault rifle, I was feeling the effects of multiple narcotics pulsing through my bloodstream. My eyes were bloodshot and blurry, and my ears were still ringing from the radiating siren. But I slowly began to realize this was no dream. As the morning light began to crack over the eastern horizon, I took my place beside Rodriguez and Murphy, and an assortment of other soldiers who were about to rush into this unfamiliar building. We had successfully completed assignments like this before, but never of this magnitude. To apprehend and capture known terrorists was the pinnacle of a soldier's career.

When the signal was given, Staff Sergeant Rodriguez barreled through the back door while I joined four other men in our unit to invade the property at a feverish speed. Murphy went first and cleared the entrance as I followed. We followed the trained routine, as we had done countless times before. But we never could have been fully prepared for the intensity of violence that would greet us over the course of the next hour.

The interior of the warehouse was dark, and our night vision goggles were limited in the advantage of seeing the heat of live images. I heard screaming from down the hallway, and gunfire from the floor above me. Murphy shouted instructions for the men behind us, still entering the door, while smoke began to fill the immediate location. I kept my back to the wall and held my rifle with my finger on the trigger, ready to explode.

Gunshots and screaming continued to ring from the floor above us, and I took my position at the end of the hallway with the agenda of securing the side door. As I neared the door, I turned to look back over my shoulder just in time to see a shadow running toward me with a handgun. I spun around and fired repeatedly, until he dropped backwards. Immediately behind him came three more insurgents, each of whom began to fire intermittently in my direction. I closed my eyes and squeezed the trigger, all the while stumbling my way in retreat... I screamed for Rodriguez, for Murphy, for anyone to help me.

In the darkness, I felt my way down the hallway until I came to another door, leading to an empty room. The gunshots continued to riddle the wall behind me, and I had no idea where the rest of the men in my unit were. My heart pounded in my chest as I searched my waistband for my communication radio. With one hand kept on my rifle and pointed in the direction of the chaos down the hallway, I turned to the frequency network of our command post. I shouted the grid coordinates of our location to the best of my blurred memory. I screamed for the assistance of reinforcements, and gave a brief description of the scene unfolding. I don't remember anything else I said, but I do remember being advised to stay calm, that help was less than two minutes away. The commanding officers at the base told me to speak more clearly, and asked for more details on the location of the enemy gunfire.

Details? For all I knew, it was raining shrapnel from the gates of hades. Bullets were shredding the walls around me, and I could hear escalating gunfire in every direction of the building. I put the radio down and waited.

My eyes were blurry, and my hands were sweating. I felt a burning sensation over my shoulder, and the fiery incense of shrapnel. I reached under my shirt and felt the source of the wound, and realized that either a bullet or an exploding piece of shrapnel had hit me. In the chaos of the preceding scene, I couldn't remember if a bomb had detonated or if it was limited to gunfire. I waited with breathless anticipation for the liberating entrance of the U.S. Army. I knew our Quick Reaction Forces were imminent, but time seemed to stand still. I heard the sound of footsteps rushing toward me, so I fled in the opposite direction. The morning light had broken into the warehouse through the shattered windows, and I could see violence in every direction.

Our mission to surprise and apprehend the terrorist network had been met with what seemed to be an anticipated response. They were ready for us, and this massive building was raining fire. My shoulder throbbed as I scurried through another open door, searching for an exit strategy.

In the distance, I saw shadows approaching my location, and I leaned back against a support beam in the corner of the main floor until they disappeared through a side door. Surrounded by the blur of gunfire and venomous screaming, I shouted again for backup. I was getting dizzy, and my breathing was choppy. But I knew that if I allowed myself to pass out, I would die. And despite all of my self-harm and indifference throughout most of my life, in that moment of facing death, I realized in the core of my being that I had a natural inclination to stay alive.

The night vision goggles were rendered dysfunctional by the time I readjusted the settings, and my fingers were dripping with sweat, so I tossed them aside and squinted into the contrast between darkness and invading daylight. I felt the internal collision of fear and adrenaline. I remembered hearing one time that you're never more alive than when you're inches from death. I was sweating, yet I was freezing. My hands were trembling, and I was beginning to feel the effect of the anxiety pills wearing off and craving the flat-line of an addiction that was my crutch.

Shots continued to ring out in the corresponding rooms adjacent to the back door. I could hear shouting in Arabic, and occasionally the familiar sound of an AR-15 assault rifle. I had no idea what had become of the other men in my unit, but I could only assume that there were multiple casualties. While I waited for reinforcements to arrive, I took an inventory of my ammunition, and looked at my watch. It seemed like an eternity had passed, but all of that violence had occurred in less than seven minutes. I reached back under my shirt and pressed against the open wound, wishing I had a way to make a tourniquet. The pain was tolerable because the nerves were offsetting the reality that I was losing a lot of blood, combined with my state of shock.

In the flash of an atomic bomb, a door kicked open and I saw two men running from across the room toward me. I picked up my assault rifle, reached for the trigger, and squeezed, spraying the entire room with bullets. Empty shell cartridges spilled to the wood floor beside me, as I continued firing. I did not relent until I saw both men drop dead in their tracks. The heat of my rifle lifted like a canon blast, and I was officially out of bullets. I could only hope that I had bought myself enough time for the backup to...

No.

In that moment, I froze in the epiphany that the men rushing toward me may very well have been coming to my rescue. *Had I fired upon my own unit?* I continued to wait for what seemed like hours, but in the immediate seconds following the shooting, I could only hear the sound of my own heart pounding. I slowly stumbled toward the two men lying prostrate before me, and as their images became clearer, my heart became numb. My worst nightmare had become a reality: the men I had mortally wounded had been coming to my rescue. American soldiers responding to the call for help, and I had unleashed friendly fire upon them.

I collapsed beside the men, deep in my own anguish. While gunfire continued to ring out from beyond the shadows, and while other men were busy screaming for help, I was lying in a frozen sweat. I looked down at their backs, and I could tell by the way that they fell that they were both dead.

Tears blurred my vision, but I stepped closer and reached down to check their pulses, just in case. The first man had taken several bullets, so I couldn't identify him. He had dropped his weapon before crashing into his final breath. I glanced over to the other man lying facedown a few feet away. I slowly moved toward him, wiping the tears from my eyes. Down the hallway, I was distracted by the sound of continued gunfire, and the shouts of my fellow infantrymen. I turned my attention back to the man on the ground before me, and turned him over to face me.

Cameron.

Chapter 7

Running For Dear Life

I ran for my life. Into the mouth of the monster, I fled from the scene into the open streets of a city suffocating in violence. I wiped the sweat from my brow, guilty stains dripping from my hands. I dropped my weapon and left the warehouse on foot, even as my fellow countrymen continued to pour into the rundown building. I heard the sound of a helicopter overheard, and in my peripheral vision I knew that the cosmic eye of a Just God was watching me.

I ran for my life. Into the belly of the beast, my exit strategy initiated a series of events that would lead to an ocean of regret. I was terrified of being found negligent, guilty, culpable (but not premeditated) and responsible for the death of two American soldiers. And Cam. Oh, God, please! Cam! The image of his body and the look of shock on his face burned into my conscience like a roman candle. I had killed my very best friend.

I ran for my life. Into the open arms of shame, each step took me deeper into the denial that my actions had fatal implications. My breath began to get heavy, and my shoulder throbbed. I was losing strength and feeling faint. "Dear God," I prayed. "I changed my mind. I don't want to see you."

The Permanent State of Disassociation

I woke up to a wave of nausea. Coughing violently, I blinked open my eyes and saw that I was surrounded by a team of doctors scurrying around to adjust my monitors. I was hooked up to variety of machines, and every time I moved, I seemed to pull the cord of my IV. An emergency nurse was checking my vitals, while a man at the foot of the bed kept asking me basic questions. "Mr. Winter, do you know what day it is?" I was still dazed by the all of the confusion. I shook my head. The questions continued. "Do you know where you are, Jordan?" I looked around the room and allowed my head to clear. My shoulder was heavily bandaged, and I realized I had just come out of surgery. "Did you get the bullet out?" I asked.

The brunette nurse continued to adjust the settings on the IV in my hand. She patted me on the arm and said, "It wasn't a bullet. We had to remove small fragments of metal... a shrapnel explosion from an Improvised Explosive Device." My head was aching, but I could not even remember an IED bomb detonating in the midst of all of the chaos and gunfire. I turned back to the doctor who was scribbling notes and asked, "How long have I been here?"

My eyes continued to adjust to the lights in the room. There were no windows in this small military hospital, but more than adequate medical care had been made available. The doctor peered up at me over his clipboard and responded, "You were brought in this morning by a military ambulance. We took you in to surgery to explore and remove as much of the shrapnel as we could. We believe we got almost all of it." He looked down at his pager as it began to vibrate on his waistband. He said he had to go, but would return as soon as he could, and several other soldiers who had been severely wounded or killed.

Later that afternoon, I would learn that the insanity of that morning had claimed the lives of nine American soldiers, and more than two dozen altogether had been wounded in the aftermath of a two-hour standoff. In what would prove to be one of the darkest hours of Operation Iraqi Freedom, the commanding officers overseeing that assignment were under intensive criticism from media pundits and scholars alike. It was a nightmare, and exposed our intelligence as sketchy at best.

I asked the nurse to increase the amount of pain medication, as my body ached from the surgery. My shoulder was elevated, and I dared not look at the wound. My body began to crave the assistance of my familiar friends—anxiety medication, pain pills, and alcohol. I repeatedly asked for morphine, because my threshold was extremely high. Throughout the night, I had flashbacks of the horror in the warehouse, repeating the visual of Cameron's body arched forward toward me.

I could not sleep. My mind raced back and forth with uncertainty. Had anyone seen the incident? Would I be held accountable or subject to investigation? And would the hospital inquiries find drugs in my system, or alcohol in my blood? I began to think of a rapid-fire response to every question that could possibly be posed to me. With every hour I withheld the truth of my actions, I fell deeper and deeper into the darkness of denial.

The next morning, I was greeted by two commanding officers that had come to visit the injured soldiers. They were respectful, and spoke quietly. They asked me how I was feeling, and if there were anything that could be done to alleviate my pain. I dared not respond honestly, because I did not know what they knew, exactly.

"Private Winter, we have come to personally thank you for your courage and service. A letter has already been circulating toward your enrollment in a medal of valor: the Purple Heart."

I could hear the awkward silence of a clock ticking on the wall behind me, and I waited for more information. Nobody spoke, so I asked, "Who were the casualties?"

I looked at both of the men, neither of them had I known

personally. The tall one, Sergeant Reed, stood up and said, "We understand that you came over here with another man from Charleston. Is that right?"

I was unsure as to whether or not this was the beginning of an inquisition, so I simply nodded. After an excruciating moment of silence, he continued, "Jordan, there were nine soldiers mortally wounded in yesterday's combat. I regret to inform you that your friend Cameron Bastian was registered in that number."

I did not say anything, nor show any emotion. I stared blankly at the wall in front of me until he continued describing the narrative. He told me about the reports of Cameron's sense of urgency to come to our assistance. It was, in fact, his passion to rush forward with the Quick Reaction Force that would inevitably have led him to his death. The more he shared, the more I realized that nobody knew that I was responsible for the bullet that ended Cam's life. My heart started to pound so rapidly, the machines monitoring my vital signs began to alarm the nurse's station.

As more of the details began to emerge, my heart continued to break. "You should know your friend Cameron had personally responded to your call for assistance. Despite multiple orders to wait for more reinforcements, he was determined to get to you. He charged into the scene without full knowledge of the situation, and was gunned down shortly after entering the main floor hallway. That's all we know."

Although my secret was safe, my heart was permanently desecrated. After the initial rush of relief swept through my veins, the reality of the narrative validated the trajectory of Cam's life. He died the way he lived—selflessly, and thinking of others. As the officers turned to leave, I saluted with stoicism. Once I could no longer hear their footsteps in the hallway, I let the tears fall. Tears of regret, shame, gratitude anger, fear, and last but not least, self-hatred.

As the wound in my shoulder began to heal, I became

increasingly anxious for my discharge. The physical therapist stopped by my hospital room twice each day and showed me the healthiest ways to move my arm without doing permanent damage. All the while, I kept wondering if there were any more investigations that could potentially connect me to the bullet that killed Cameron. As far as I was concerned, no news was good news.

After eleven days in the hospital, I was cleared for discharge. Chaplain Acheson surprised me with a visit the morning I was getting ready to leave. He said he only wanted to be "a non-anxious presence" for me. But somehow, his quiet demeanor only made me more worried. It was as if he could see through me and straight into my conscience, and knew the truth. I must have presented a guilty disposition, because I was fidgeting and not making eye contact with him while trying to collect my personal items. "Jordan," he said, "Are you doing okay?"

I blinked at him in disbelief. Was I doing okay? What kind of a question was that? I just spent the past eleven days in hospital physically recovering from an incident that I would never recover from emotionally. My finger pulled the trigger that unleashed a bullet that killed my best friend, and to make matters worse, at the time of the tragedy, I was under the influence of drugs and alcohol. "No, sir," I said slowly. "I am not okay."

He did not stand up or look away. He pondered my answer for a moment and then quietly said, "It's okay to not be okay."

I was anticipating him to give me a cliché bible verse or motivational pat on the back. I assumed he was coming to give me a comprehensive answer to the mystery of God's orchestration in recent events. I couldn't look at him, because I was too afraid of somehow saying too much and blowing my secret conviction. "Is this the part where you're gonna tell me that God has a plan for all of this and that everything happens for a reason and stuff?"

The chaplain did not flinch in his immediate response. "God

does have a plan, Jordan. And, no, it wasn't this." He remained calm, yet convinced. "God's original plan was a garden of shalom... peace, on earth as it is in heaven. But once His own created order that began to rebel from that plan, an alternative spin was unleashed." In just a few paragraphs, he described the downward spiral of humanity into a cancerous sin that has resulted with a fatal virus on the created order. I thought about the images of war I had witnessed firsthand and contributed to. I thought about the death of innocence and the execution of my optimism.

Once I was officially discharged from the hospital, Chaplain Acheson personally transported me back to the base, where several officers greeted me as we parked at the front entrance of the Administration Building. I was advised to report to the Colonel's office upon arrival. Other men in the unit began to hoot and cheer when I walked from the vehicle toward the front doors. I wasn't sure what was happening, or if it were some kind of joke. I followed the Chaplain into the Colonel's office and took a seat beside him.

"Good morning, Private Winter," he greeted me, shaking my hand. I saluted back respectfully and replied, "Sir, good morning, sir!" My heart continued to pound in my chest until he motioned for me to relax. I looked at Chaplain Acheson for reassurance, and waited for the Colonel to speak. He handed me an envelope. "First of all, I want to personally thank you for your heroic efforts to serve the United States at home and abroad. Your peers, as well as your commanding officers, have validated your courage. It has not gone unnoticed."

He told me to open the envelope. My hands were trembling as I attempted to open the content with one hand, while my other hand remained motionless from the sling holding my shoulder in place. I fumbled around for a moment, struggling to open the letter, until Chaplain Acheson finally reached over to assist me. He pulled out a printed letter with an official seal from the United States Army. The Colonel interrupted my stream of consciousness by saying, "You've been nominated and approved for the Purple Heart, Jordan."

A Purple Heart is one of the highest honors a soldier can earn, awarded for his or her courage in active combat, specifically to the point of being wounded in war. It was an award that should have no association to Jordan Winter. Throughout the events of the past few weeks, I had become emotionally depleted and despondent. But as I held this letter, and the corresponding benefits of an award for which I was unworthy, I almost fainted.

I slowly leaned against Chaplain Acheson until my head was supported against his shoulder. He wrapped his arm around me and said, "It's okay, Jordan. I know you're feeling overwhelmed with all of this right now. You're grieving the loss of your best friend, and you're also still in a lot of physical pain too. The combination of emotional and physical trauma can be catastrophic, so it's important that you let us help you." My ears began to drown out the words of affirmation and the accolades of "We're so proud of you," and "Your courage is honorable"… if only they knew I was nothing more than a drug addict who fled from reality through the coping mechanisms of pharmaceutical assistance, and I was a coward who was running from the truth.

Somehow, I managed to collect my emotions and politely thank the officers. As I stood to leave, the Colonel walked me to the door. "In the next few days, you'll be contacted by our resident grief counselors, as well as an advisory committee assigned to review the details of your last engagement. Meanwhile, please get some rest."

I walked back to my locker and clawed through my belongings. I began to retrace my steps and cover my tracks if at all possible. Whatever pills I had remaining were crushed and flushed down the toilet. And I verified that I had no more vodka camouflaged in the mouthwash. I deleted contacts in my phone, and erased text messages. Every hint of my reproach was hidden to the best of my ability. The paranoia of being discovered negligent at the time of Cam's death was suffocating me. I purged my locker and flushed away every piece of evidence I could.

Honorable Discharge

The following Tuesday morning, I was summoned to meet with an advisory committee assigned to my status. Once again, I had no idea what to expect going into the meeting, but when I arrived, the first two faces I saw were Chaplain Acheson and Dr. Pavlock. I took a seat at a large table across from them and four other commanding officers and waited for them to speak.

After an initial informal greeting, one of the commanding officers, Sergeant Morris, reviewed my medical records. "Considering the scope of your injury, it has been advised you be removed from any role in active combat. Obviously, your shoulder is going to need intensive physical therapy, and by the time you are presumed ready to return, your enlistment dates will have expired."

I stared straight ahead through the open window, out toward the rising sun. As all of the implications of my injury were beginning to sink into my psyche, Sergeant Morris continued. "As it turns out, there is a Warrior Transitional Unit near Columbia, where you attended basic training. This committee has agreed you will be assigned to that unit, where you will begin the acclimation to civilian life, while being heavily monitored by physical and mental health professionals."

Another commanding officer added additional details. My transition would be effective immediately, and would allow for me to be "surrounded by friends and family" just a short drive from Charleston. I could spend most of my time back home, as long as I reported on weekends to the central office in Columbia.

Chaplain Acheson interrupted a long pause, taking the

conversation in another direction. "You came here together, shoulder to shoulder with your best friend, correct?" I looked at him and nodded, knowing he already knew this. His eyes seemed to smile as he winked at me and said, "How would you like to leave the same way you came?" I raised my eyebrow incredulously, unsure as to what exactly he meant. Sergeant Morris picked up the conversation and said, "Jordan, how would you like to serve as an official escort of Cameron's body back to his memorial service in Charleston?"

To be honest, I was torn between incomprehensible joy and nuclear sadness. There would have been no greater honor than to walk beside my friend one last time, if it had not been for the reality that I was the reason he was in the casket. Unable to articulate my feelings, I rubbed at my forehead as if to chase away a migraine that had been gaining momentum for an entire lifetime.

My arm would remain in a sling for another six weeks, as the surgery involved extensive tissue removal. I nodded and said, "I understand. But what do I do until then? Where does that leave me?"

Sergeant Morris handed me a letter with another official signature. "You're being granted an honorable discharge, with a medal of valiant courage... the Purple Heart." This letter was my official notice of discharge, clearing me of any further responsibilities to the United States Army. I was being sent home, to rebuild my life.

I looked at Chaplain Acheson for affirmation, and he patted me on the shoulder, but didn't say anything. From across the table, Dr. Pavlock inquired, "How are feeling right now, Jordan? Does this come as a surprise? Are you relieved?"

I glanced down at the letter, trying to wrap my mind around the implications of being set free from the bondage of this place. I was more than relieved—I was ecstatic. "Yes!" I said. "I just want to go home!" Dr. Pavlock told me I would need to follow a detailed treatment plan for both my physical and mental recovery. He would collaborate with my doctors and psychiatric professionals in Charleston to provide continued evaluation and support.

I stood to my feet, holding my official letter of release. As the honorary discharge continued to sink into my brain, all I could think about was packing up and going home. I was granted permission to leave at any time, and I wanted to leave right that very minute. As I exited the room, I saluted the commanding officers, and shook hands with Chaplain Acheson. "Please pray for me," I said. "God and I have a few things to sort through."

Once back at my room, I took a quick inventory and realized the majority of my possessions were specific to my involvement in the war. I had to go through a series of checklists, turning in and accounting for all of my weapons. I still had no idea whatever happened to the rifle I had dropped at the time of the shooting. I never mentioned it, and I was never asked about the specifics. For all I know, Al-Qaeda soldiers may have retrieved it. The most difficult part of packing to leave was discerning the difference between what things belonged to me personally and what would remain Army property. In some ways, I felt like I was a piece of property that had used violently by my own government.

Almost everything I owned could fit into an oversized suitcase. I crammed my clothes, pillow, a few books, and my journal inside and tugged at the zipper until it was secure. I set the suitcase beside my bed, so that I would be ready to leave at dawn's first light.

In less than twelve hours, Cameron Bastian's lifeless body would be placed into a coffin and depart for Charleston. I would be buckled on the same flight, escorting my friend back to his people.

Chapter 8

A Bleeding, Purple Heart

If it weren't for my travel bag, I would have been early to the airport. The oversized luggage came equipped with four wheels, one of which was permanently locked and refused to roll. I ended up dragging the ridiculous-looking trunk around a crowded airport, yanking it loose from every possible snag along the way. At my layover in Baltimore, I became increasingly aware of the attention given to my uniform. Elderly gentlemen saluted me, and teenage girls whispered, staring at my uniform. Single moms pointed out my military patches to their small children. I was a decorated combat veteran, and with my arm in a sling, people took notice. I didn't make eye contact with anyone, pretended not to hear their words of affirmation around each corner. Under my breath, I cursed the broken wheel on my suitcase of shame. It was only fitting that I should have to drag around the remains of who I was in a container that was about to explode.

Military officials concerned themselves with the transfer of Cameron's casket from the plane, and I would not be reunited with him again until his memorial service the following afternoon. I turned my attention to securing my luggage and getting out of the crowded vicinity as quickly as possible.

Apparently a liaison officer from the Army had contacted my mother to let her know about my discharge, because by the time my plane touched down in Charleston, she had been waiting for several hours. Although our military tenure had been brief, the local news broadcasts had been anxious to run a story about Cameron's death and my "heroic" return. I took my place in line to exit the plane with a multitude of other passengers. As soon as my mother saw me, she shouted my name over the commotion. I was surprised to see her, and I didn't know how much she had heard about Cameron's death.

"Mom!" I said, reaching for a hug. "How did you know I was coming home?" She was caught in that mysterious vortex between crying and laughter. Her words were flustered, and she squeezed me tightly until she realized my arm was still in a sling. "Oh, Jordan, I'm so glad you're home safe! It's all over now, no more bullets and no more God-awful bombs!" We stepped aside so the line behind us could get by, and then we slowly followed the crowd down the hallway. As we walked, my mother explained how she had received a phone call from someone from the Community Relations office and was simply told I had been injured, but expected to recover, and I was coming home.

I was quite distracted by the culture shock of returning to a modern airport. Cinnabon and Starbucks filled the air, as white-collared businessmen talked on their cell phones. I could see my mother's mouth moving as she talked, but I was having a hard time hearing her words. I nodded slowly, pretending to actively listen as I dragged my suitcase around like a rebellious dog on a strained leash.

As we neared the automatic exit doors, I noticed television cameras and a news broadcast team crowded near the exit. My mom pulled on my shirt and said, "They've been calling the house hoping to interview you, Jordan."

"Interview me?" I asked, incredulously. "Why?" My mother shrugged and explained the story circulating through local channels: that there had been a violent firefight in Baghdad, claiming the life of nearly a dozen American soldiers, including Cameron Bastian. After a brief pause, she added, "And that Jordan Winter is returning home with a Purple Heart, which he nobly earned from the wounds he sustained in active combat."

"So, I'm a hero, huh?" I mumbled quietly. "Let's get out of here, Mom. Is there another exit?" I looked around aggressively for a way around the news cameras and microphones. There was no way I was about to agree to a news interview, or milk the attention. All I wanted to do was hide. I turned around and backtracked quickly into the airport, with one arm dragging around a broken suitcase full of disgrace, my mother trailing behind me. We walked to the far corridor and out the side doors, down the sidewalk toward the parking garage where my mother had left the truck. I looked over my shoulder as we walked away, anxious to get on the highway.

Once we made it safely back to my apartment, I took the phone off the receiver and lowered the shades. "Whatever you do, Mom," I said, "Don't answer the phone or the door. I don't want to see or talk to anyone." She rubbed my back and said soothingly, "I understand, honey. You're home now. Just relax and focus on getting better. Let me make you something to eat. Are you hungry?"

I explained to her that I was given clearance to attend Cam's memorial service, but that I was required to report in to the Warrior Transitional Unit in Columbia the following Monday. Once I was psychologically cleared, I would return home and report back on the weekends. We talked in fragmented sentences about the past several months and about the tragic realities of war.

Later that evening, my mother informed me that Cameron's memorial service was scheduled for the following morning. His casket was carried from the plane, and the news clips continued to play the video loop of his homecoming. I kept the television muted, but I watched as the images repeated. Cam's casket was covered with an oversized American flag, and his profile picture kept flashing on the screen.

I sat motionless on the couch as my mother tried to console me. I didn't even hear a word she said. All I could think about was how badly I wished it had been me in the casket, not Cameron. I finally knew the true meaning of the term survivor's guilt I stared blankly at the television screen until my eyelids grew heavy and eventually fluttered closed. That night, my mother fell asleep in the chair beside the couch, where I dreamed it had all been a nightmare.

In Memoriam

My closet was crammed full of old shirts and stained jeans. I didn't even own a tie, let alone a black suit that would have been appropriate attire for my best friend's funeral service. The unspoken rule is that a soldier granted an honorary discharge from active duty should wear his military uniform, but I did not want any attention whatsoever. My mother drove us into town so I could buy some new clothes, and I picked out a pair of dress pants and a woven shirt that would suffice as an honorable goodbye to my best friend.

I should have known to arrive early to find a seat, but even thirty minutes before the memorial service was scheduled to begin, traffic was backed up as people slowly searched for parking. Local police officers were directing traffic to and from the busy intersection, motioning for my mother to enter the crowded parking lot adjacent to the funeral home. I sat in the passenger seat, avoiding eye contact with the officer conducting traffic. I remembered him from the time he had arrested me for driving under the influence two years prior.

Once inside the main auditorium, I felt my anxiety escalating quickly. This was my first time in town since I'd arrived home, and the series of events from the past several days had left me emotionally depleted. My mother walked beside me as I stayed as close to the wall as possible, walking quickly toward the last row in the overflow seating room. My arm remained in a sling, and my eyes bounced to the seats around me, refusing to make contact with anyone who might be staring in my direction.

From the back row, I could see the crowd continuing to file in. From my peripheral vision, I felt the discomfort of an intense stare. I looked to my left and saw Sierra's friend, Cassie, whom I hadn't seen since Thanksgiving morning, when I had left her silently on the couch in Sierra's living room. She waved at me, but I just looked away, pretending not to see her.

News of Cameron's death had absolutely decimated our community. He was the beloved son of a well-known family in Charleston, symbolically adopted as the local hero who had gone off to defend our freedom. In the front of the auditorium was a closed casket with a massive American flag draped over the top of it. Above the casket was a large projector screen with moving images of Cam's life. As music softly played, pictures displayed a story of a life well-lived. A small blonde boy beaming in a red wagon, awkward middle school pictures of little league baseball and a participation trophy, varsity football and Homecoming King... all of the pictures brought sighs and laughter and tears from the crowd, now standing room only.

As the pictures built a chapter story of Cameron's life, it was clear that a certain girl had always captured his heart. There were beautiful memories preserved in moments frozen in time: senior prom, Sierra pinning a corsage on Cam's tuxedo, another picture of them on the dance floor, and then another picture of Sierra spraying him with a garden hose while he retaliated with a squirt gun.

But there was one picture that absolutely wrecked me. It was a picture of the three of us, sitting on the beach beside a bonfire. The image captured me focused on roasting a fluffy white marshmallow over the flame, while Cam smiled back at the camera. He had his arm around me, and I didn't even realize it. Sitting next to Cameron was Sierra, gazing up at him with inexplicable adoration. She had loved him with all of her heart, mind, and soul.

Scattered throughout the attendance emanated audible sobs when, from the side entrance, Cameron's widow entered the room. Sierra was wearing a purple dress, and she carried a red rose. She walked first to the casket, placed the rose on the flag, and sat down next to Cam's parents in the front row. And that's when I almost fell to the ground in anguish. My heart was shattered for her! Even as the music continued, the uncontrollable sobbing continued from those who knew Cameron the best. His mother cried in the arms of his father, who held her close.

Cameron and Sierra's pastor, Pastor Ryan, welcomed everyone on behalf of the family, and thanked the community for the overwhelming support in recent days. He shared stories of neighbors, even strangers, who had written cards and brought groceries to the Bastian family.

The eulogy included the famous passage from Psalm 23, and the pastor focused his attention by concluding even after walking "through the valley of the shadow of death, surely grace and mercy follow me…" He mentioned that the original Hebrew translation for "follow" would have actually been "hunted."

"Putting that all in context," he said, "Despite the travails of life and death, God's grace and mercy hunts me down!"

I imagined the idea of looking over my shoulder for the wrath of God against my secret shame, only to be apprehended by a cosmic grace that transcends the legal code of my conscious torment. And I wanted so desperately for this grace to be true for me.

At the conclusion of the memorial service, Pastor Ryan asked the community to pray for Sierra, who, after hearing of the tragic death of her husband, had been stricken with a paralyzing grief that sent her into premature labor. She was rushed to the hospital and with the incredible care provided by the Birthing Unit and gave birth to a premature baby girl.

"Let us honor Cam by lifting up his wife and daughter during this difficult time..." Pastor Blevins said.

My mother looked at me, and I stared straight ahead. I was trying to get a glimpse of Sierra, but there were too many people in the way. This was all news to me, as I had not even thought about the health of the baby in the midst of this emotional agony. Pastor Ryan continued to articulate that Sierra had come to the funeral service this morning directly from the Neonatal Infant Care Unit of Saint Luke's Regional Hospital.

"Babies who are born prematurely are at a higher risk of brain and other neurological complications, as well as breathing and digestive problems. At this time, Sierra's baby is stable, but she is undergoing continued testing and intensive care. Please continue to pray for this entire family."

Throughout the memorial service, Sierra remained calm. She looked only at the casket in front of her, and even when Cameron's father gave the closing prayer, she kept her eyes fixated on the flag covering his body. I felt as if I could feel her breathing, paradoxically, and suddenly I felt a million miles away.

After the service, Sierra stood with Cameron's family in front of the casket, as an estimated crowd of one thousand mourners waited in line to offer their condolences. One after another, hugs were followed by soft whispers, followed by tears and awkwardly slow progressions past the casket. I waited for what seemed like hours for my opportunity to see her, but the closer I stepped in her direction, the heavier my heart became. I asked my mother if she could find another ride home, and whispered, "I have to get out of here."

My entire life, I had always battled anxiety, but this was different... this was shame. Toxic shame. Crippling shame. Suffocating shame. Suicidal shame. Knock-me-off-my feet shame.

Incomprehensible shame. Violent shame. Inside out shame. Upside-down shame. Runaway shame. Hide-in-the-closet shame.

I looked around for the nearest exit and found the side door. It was the same door Sierra entered an hour earlier. I disappeared into the suffocating oblivion of self-hatred.

Chapter 9

Blessed Are the
Spiritually Bankrupt

M y hands gripped the steering wheel and my foot hit the accelerator, and I tore out of there like a like a lion loosed from his cage. I squealed the tires, kicking up smoke in the rearview mirror as I fled the scene. Gasping for air, I turned on the defroster as the February ice crashed into my conscience like a freight train. I was completely blinded by my fear, and polarized thinking distorted my cognition. Stop signs became invitations for insurrection. Red lights became seductive solicitations for accelerated rebellion.

The highway was empty, and my anxiety faded into a manic depression. I drove for hours, going west, chasing the daylight. I turned my cell phone off and turned up the radio as the Kings of Leon screamed at me to loosen my tie. I took the back roads and the rural routes, preferring anonymity. As far as I was concerned, I never wanted to be seen again. My mental state was deteriorating to the point of illness; such was the aftermath of considering my options. In my distorted cognition, I was a character in *The Matrix*, choosing to swallow the blue pill, with eyes opened to the reality the blood of an innocent man had stained my guilty hands, and the cosmic judge had sentenced me to life in the prison of my own regret. I was literally shaking from the sickness within as my eyes scanned the horizon for the nearest exit. I didn't know where I was going, and I didn't care.

Somewhere deep in the pocket of a no-name town, I found the skeleton of a truck stop, the remains of an abandoned gas station. There appeared to be no sign of life, or even running electricity, for many miles. And long after the sun had set, I was left alone with runaway tears and white knuckles sweating in the freezing cold. My fuel tank was near empty, but I could not drive any farther. Besides, I had nowhere to go. So I pulled to a stop in a parking lot with broken concrete and invasive weeds.

Just when I thought I had reached the end of my rope, rock bottom seemed to have a black hole in the basement floor. My fear and self-hatred had emerged into a lethal depression, inescapable. Thoughts flooded in from the fountain of shame, an intrinsic current of self-harm. I wanted to punish myself and be put out of my own misery. I wanted to end this cycle of addiction, escape, and relapse. I wanted to be set free from the negative emotions that had been tormenting me for as long as I could remember, but I didn't know how to break myself from the chain.

I was freezing, and my fuel light started flashing. I stepped out of the car into the midnight wind, the frigid wind cutting through my jacket as if I were naked. I opened the trunk to rummage through a few old bags until I found a blanket and another old jacket, and tucked just underneath the jacket was a Phillips screwdriver. I held it in my hand and stood still for a minute, contemplating this tool as a weapon of self-destruction.

I climbed into the backseat of my car, wrapping myself in the blanket and leaving the car running with the heat on high. Any minute, I thought, and the engine would cough out. The gasoline had been running practically on fumes for almost an hour. I gripped the screwdriver with my right hand and looked up at the moon, hiding behind thick clouds. And I began to cry because *I knew I was serious this time*, I was inches from suicide.

The first cut across my left forearm seemed to burn like a scalding oven, as my arm began to feel the flames of justice. The cut wasn't fatal, but just deep enough to unleash the adrenaline of the some glad morning and the unbroken circle and the sweet by and by and Do Lord, please remember me as I knock on your door, repeatedly and ashamedly. Once I felt like I had punished myself sufficiently, I dropped the screwdriver and held my raging arm out toward God, and the True North that seemed transcendent, detached, and a million miles away.

My mind was exhausted and my body was still on Baghdad time, so I fell asleep in the midst of excruciating pain. It was too dark to see the self-inflicted wounds on my left arm and I was too cold to feel anything, but when I woke up in the morning, I saw the aftermath. The blanket was soaked but I slept through the pain, and I woke up in a blur of confusion. But when I opened my eyes, I felt deadness on the inside. I was numb.

At some point throughout the night, my car had sputtered and then turned off. I tried to start my car to reignite the heat, but then remembered that I had officially run out of gas. Although I had always heard biblical descriptions of hell as a lake of fire, it seemed I'd been banished to an eternity here, in a vacant parking lot in the February cold, dripping with guilt.

I curled up in the backseat in the fetal position, trying to retain my body heat by rubbing my hands together and breathing on them. My breath came out in cold puffs, hung in the morning air like a question without an answer to a God who seemed like an ever-present absence.

Nevertheless, from this platform of obvious ruin, I stretched my right arm toward heaven. Chaplain Acheson once said that when you don't know how to pray, the Holy Spirit can interpret our tears as a heavenly language. So I groaned for God to rescue me. I looked up toward the leafless trees, and wondered if my ache had a volume one octave too high for recollection. "God. Oh, God!" I prayed only those words, repeatedly.

Whatever *this* is… a breaking point, an epiphany from spiritual enlightenment, or a moment of crisis that leads to salvation, had led me to a place of genuine surrender. And all of those self-help books had no remedy. No amount of self-confidence could get me out of this pit of despair. I was not embracing the philosophy of "self-love" or the shameless self-promotion born in the sewage of humanism. I felt ruined, and drowning, and in need of a rescue. If ever there was a guilty verdict, it was in the backseat of a rusty Jeep, empty of fuel and nearly frozen to death.

A few hours later, I tied my shoes and zipped up my jacket and slowly stepped out the door. I walked nearly three miles off the main road before I saw a single car pass by. I tried to raise my arms and motion for roadside assistance, but the vehicle zoomed past me as if I were invisible. I walked quickly and deliberately back toward the highway. I had no legitimate clue where I was, exactly. From the mile marker I passed, I realized I had driven almost 300 miles west, so I marched like a dedicated soldier for several miles until the oncoming traffic increased. I raised my thumb and stuck out my arm, the cuts on my arm were covered by a faded jacket.

Eventually, a man in a Dodge truck pulled over to assist me. He had noticed my arm still in a sling, and wanted to make sure if I needed any help. As it turned out, I was quite a ways from the next exit, but he offered to drive me to and from town, where I was able to get a portable gas transport. He drove me all the way back to the vacant parking lot, mumbling under his breath all the while. "You must have been seriously lost to end up out in these parts. This is no man's land here."

He had no idea just how lost I really was.

He rolled down his window and watched as I poured the gasoline into my fuel tank. After starting my ignition, he nodded and pulled away. I waved gratefully, and promised to pay it forward someday. Upon starting the car, I immediately cranked the heat up and rubbed my hands over the heater, waiting for the relief of warmth. I turned on the radio, and listened to a radio jockey discuss the plummeting temperatures, advising motorists to drive carefully through patches of dry ice and moderate snow flurries.

But none of that scared me. Somehow, surviving bullets and shrapnel have a way of making everything else seem like kindergarten. I turned left, and then right, to get back on the rural highway, stopping only once to load up on fuel and coffee. I gulped the steaming coffee, realizing that I had gone almost 24 hours without food or water. The caffeine flooded my veins, and although my arm had stopped bleeding, it was throbbing in outrage at my desecration.

As I drove onward, I had only one thought: Sierra. The images of her pictures at Cameron's funeral still burned into my memory like a tattoo on my brain. My heart was truly broken for her, and I knew what I had to do. Whatever the cost of her baby's medical bills, I would make sure everything was taken care of. Whatever home renovations she needed, I would personally do myself. I began to make a mental checklist of how I would devote my time and energy toward helping her. She would never have to mow her own lawn or scrape ice from her windshield for the rest of her life. There would never be an outsourced, overpriced contractor paid to repair her appliances or finish the shingles on her roof. I was going to look out for Cam's family, and be the guardian angel that he had always been for me.

Much of my ambition was laced in my own emotional processing of redemption. I felt like the only way that I could ever forgive myself would be to work hard and earn it. I was going to focus all of my physical, mental, and spiritual energy on taking care of Sierra and her baby. As I drove eastward, the sun was still rising, and as my thoughts drifted toward the blueprints of a constructed future, the palm trees of eastern South Carolina shimmered in my peripheral vision. I clutched my cup of coffee long after it was depleted, and I realized that I was like an empty cup myself, being held in the hand of a merciful God.

Construction rerouted all highway traffic as I neared Charleston, and I took the detour off the rural route toward a parallel road that would connect me closer to Saint Luke's Regional Hospital. By the time I arrived, the afternoon shadows threatened rain, but none would come. I continued to rehearse my imminent greeting to Sierra. How had I not yet spoken with her during the most traumatic time of her life? When I was standing in line at the funeral, all I wanted to do was pull her aside from the crowd so we could grieve in private. But I didn't. I couldn't. I was selfish, and I didn't want to share her with a room full of acquaintances. I would have given anything to whisk her away to the beach, and open up to her about everything that happened… but therein was buried a tension so deep that it would require open heart surgery to remove.

I parked in the visitor lot across the street and followed the signs to the Neonatal Intensive Care Unit. Walking through the winding hallways, I prepared myself to be introduced to the infant daughter that was born from the romance of my two best friends. I opted to take the stairs up five flights, feeling unworthy to be lifted by an elevator. As I climbed the steps, my heart began to beat more quickly, and I was losing the air in my lungs as I got each step closer to the painful sight of my best friend's grieving widow.

I stopped at the nurses' station to ask for directions. An elderly nurse looked up from the computer monitor. "Can I help you, sir?" I suddenly felt like she could see through my shirt and jacket, straight to the colorful evidence of last night's cutting. I looked down at my arm and realized that I had not yet bandaged it, and I hoped that it went unseen.

"I'm looking for Sierra Bastian's room, please." I shaped the statement into an interrogative, and listened intently to the instructions: Around the corner, down the hall… room 5312.

I looked down at my feet as my steps carried me toward her. I could hear babies crying intermittently as I passed through the Birthing Unit, and I wondered if any of those lungs belonged to Sierra's daughter. As I approached the door, I collected my emotions and fell silent. There were no words... despite the millions of thoughts running through my head, I could not find the appropriate assortment of vocabulary.

I'm sorry. I'm here.

I was lost. It is all my fault.

I killed him. I killed me, too.

I ran away. I ran home.

Where is home? Sierra.

These were my scattered thoughts, but all I could do was stand there in the doorway and cry. The door was propped open, and I could see Sierra with her back to me. She was still wearing her purple dress and black dress shoes from the funeral. I couldn't remember the last time I saw her with shoes on. It's strange how the mind begins to drift from the present moment. Sierra was standing and looking out the window quietly, holding a delicate treasure in her arms. I don't know how long I stood there, with tears running down my face... but my paralytic speech was confronted by Sierra's voice.

"Jordan," she said, still facing the window. "Where have you been?"

I wasn't sure how she knew I was standing there, if it was just her intuition. I found out later that she had seen me standing in the doorway through the reflection in the window pane. I stood frozen in the moment, and instinctively replied the familiar refrain: "I've been up to no good, Sierra."

She turned toward me as I walked through the door. She was carrying her infant daughter in a pink blanket, wrapped tightly in her arms. Sierra approached me and leaned into my chest, as I put my right arm around her. My left arm was still in a sling, and her arms were full of love. We stood there, both of us crying, with no words. In the background, I could still hear the faint crying of newborn babies struggling to operate new, unfamiliar lungs.

Sierra looked up at me, a runaway tear captured by gravity. "Let me introduce you to Karis, Jordan." She lifted up her arms to offer a closer glimpse of her baby daughter. I held out my own to receive the gift, pulling her close to my chest with one arm. She couldn't have been more than four pounds of adorability, wrapped in a pink blanket. Her eyes opened for a moment, and she closed them quickly before scowling her eyebrows. Too much light, apparently. So I covered her back up with the blanket, and said softly, "Hello, Karis."

"Her name is loaded with meaning," Sierra said. "Karis means 'grace.'"

There were two chairs facing each other in the corner of the room. I sat down next to Sierra, as I held Karis, and listened to her describe the brutal moments of her darkest hour, when she'd heard of Cam's death. "I was sitting out on the porch, early in the morning. I had just brewed some hot tea and I sat down to read through the Proverbs... You know how there are thirty-one days in a typical month? Well, there are also thirty-one chapters in the Old Testament book of Proverbs. So Cameron and I had agreed to read the corresponding chapter of each day, even in our separate locations. I had just finished the chapter and closed my eyes to pray, but when I looked up, there was a government-issued vehicle pulling into the driveway."

She turned from the window to look down at her feet. Karis

stirred briefly in my arms, but fell back asleep a few seconds later. Sierra continued, "I knew immediately that they had come to tell me about Cam. I don't even remember what they said… two men in uniform stood with me on the porch, as I fell to my knees, devastated. They were so gentle, and tried to be soothing, but all I could think about was being a single mother."

Sierra fluctuated between tears and laughter, recalling the awkwardness of her water breaking as she sobbed on the front porch. "I cried so violently that it sent my body into premature labor," she said. "You should have seen the look on their faces when my water broke."

She went on to describe the voluntary transport to the hospital, and the horrific pain of natural childbirth. It had all happened so quickly, she didn't even have time for the epidural shot. "I nearly passed out in the delivery. I was watching closely the look on the doctor's faces as they scrambled to provide care for Karis. She wasn't breathing on her own at first." Sierra paused. "They took her away and began to work on her lungs. As it turns out, the stress in the delivery and the lack of oxygen might have contributed to her diagnosis."

Karis had been diagnosed with Chiari Malformation, an abnormality in the brain that extended into the spinal canal. While this medical condition was typically not life threatening, it could affect her quality of life in the future, specifically related to frequent migraine headaches, poor neurological motor skills, and coordination. Sierra described the immaculate care provided by dedicated nurses here in the Neonatal Intensive Care Unit. "All of the tests, reports, and evaluations seem to indicate she's going to be just fine." Although her vitals and major organs were fully functioning, the research had suggested that more evaluation would be needed, with ongoing analysis.

I stood up and carried Karis over to Sierra. "Listen to me, Sierra." She reached out and I handed her baby back to her. "I've come to tell you I'm not leaving. I'm staying right here where I belong. You are the only family that I have, and this is my home."

I promised her that I was going to take care of things around the house. In honor of Cam, I would look after his family—it was the least that I could do, considering I was the one who was directly responsible. I looked down at her as she put a blanket over her chest, nursing Karis with maternal care. Sierra didn't say anything, just looked up at me in the paradox of smiling tears, and I was dismantled with love for her.

Chapter 10

Wounded Warrior

Two weeks later, I was commissioned to report in person to the regional Warrior Transitional Unit in Columbia. This appointed season was a part of the Army's response to a growing number of soldiers who had returned from active combat bringing the demons of war home with them. The vastness of psychological damage, Post-Traumatic Stress Disorder, and sinister violence had proven to take a toll on returning soldiers struggling to readjust to civilian life. How does a man adjust from being trained and celebrated as a killing machine to controlling his road rage in Charleston's rush hour traffic?

However polarizing the war in the Middle East had become, I was not neutral. The awards given to me upon my exit from the military were neither embraced nor celebrated by my conscience. I felt neither honorable in my discharge, nor courageous in my combat. I knew my heart, my *real* heart, was not purple—it was some other fusion of colors compiled of ashes and scar tissue. I thought little about the men I had mortally wounded in combat, or their wives and children. I deleted the horrific scenes of decapitation, mass execution, and exaggerated violence from my memory. I would find out over the years that memory loss is a common side effect of PTSD, and that I was not alone.

But I sure felt alone. As I waited in line to be registered to the

Transitional Unit, my memory conjured up the last time I'd been here. Cameron and I had just graduated from Basic Training, and I remember feeling in sync with the universe. I remembered the children's choir singing at the ceremony, the peaceful hymns, and the sense of anticipation. My thoughts lingered over that memory for a brief minute, as I remembered how optimistic I was made to feel. I stared out the window, lost in thought until a receptionist called my name. "Jordan Winter."

I blinked back to the present moment, then stood and picked up my backpack, still loaded with all of personal items from Baghdad. All of my paperwork and military identification was inside, as well as my journal and a few pictures. "I'm here," I said.

"Do you have your ID with you?" an elderly woman asked from behind the counter. I took off my backpack and opened it up, pulling out an envelope full of important documents. I handed her everything I had, and hoped that she could help me make sense of the mess I'd made. She checked her computer screen and nodded, "You've been assigned to Dr. Bailey. Her office is on the third floor, room 318. You can take the elevator down the hall to your left."

I nodded. Here we go. Another detached doctor. As it turned out, the chief objective of this Warrior Transitional Unit is to gauge the mental health of soldiers who are returning to civilian life after active combat. And where there is significant psychological trauma, expert clinicians are assigned to provide cognitive behavioral therapy. It wasn't that I didn't agree with the importance of properly processing the overwhelming torment and guilt that survivors must feel; it's just that I didn't want to talk about it. At least not to this Dr. Bailey, who'd probably never been in a fistfight her entire life, let alone had to claw out the pieces of exploding shrapnel from her shoulder.

I found my way to room 318, and stood before a door that was cracked open. Before I could even knock, I heard a gentle voice call me inside. "Come on in, Jordan." I looked over my shoulder, although I knew she was talking to me. I opened the door and stepped inside. Although I had been expecting to find a crotchety old scientist in a lab coat, a beautiful, young therapist warmly welcomed me. She stood up from behind her desk and walked toward me, extending her hand. "Hi, Jordan, I'm Dr. Bailey. I'm glad you made it. Please, have a seat." She motioned for me to sit down on the couch while she reclined in the chair next to it.

The first thing I noticed was her long, auburn hair. She had a beauty mark on her cheek, and a kind smile. I felt better already. I looked around the room and saw her various degrees emphasizing abnormal psychology. This, of course, seemed appropriate, because I was anything but normal. Dr. Bailey held a notepad on her lap and initiated the conversation by telling me Dr. Pavlock had sent her my files with my consent. "It's obvious you've seen almost everything imaginable," she said. "I have sufficient documentation for the past couple of years, but absolutely nothing before your military record. So I am very interested to learn about the foundational years that have helped to shape you into the man you are today."

I must have missed my cue to launch into the full autobiographical account, because Dr. Bailey waited in silence for a short while before she prompted, "So, tell me how you ended up here."

Chaplain Acheson once told me that I had a knack for sarcasm. This explains why I flippantly shrugged my shoulders and said, "Well, I killed a bunch of people and stuff. So there's that."

"You killed a bunch of people and stuff," Dr. Bailey repeated, nodding. She must have been trading notes with Chaplain Acheson, because then she added, "You know many people believe sarcasm is just a coping mechanism for emotional exhaustion. Do you think that's true of you?"

I looked at her and smiled, putting my feet up on the couch.

"Is this the part where I'm supposed to lay my head back and tell you all about my abusive father?"

Without missing a beat, Dr. Bailey asked, "*Was* your father abusive?"

"No, he was just a jerk," I said. "Were you abused as a child, Dr. Bailey?"

"Yes, actually, I was," she said, not flinching. I certainly didn't expect that.

We both sat in silence for a minute, and then Dr. Bailey stood up and walked toward the window, opening it up so the fresh air could circulate throughout the room. From across the floor, she said, "I read in your file that your best friend was killed on a combat mission with you. I'm sorry to hear that, Jordan." I was curious just what exactly was in my file about the incident, but I didn't say anything.

"Did you see it happen?" she inquired, as she walked slowly back to her chair next to me. I looked down at the floor and gave the most honest answer I could: "It was all a blur."

She noticed my arm was still in a sling, as my physical therapy required minimal movement. "And the shrapnel in your right shoulder...did they get it all out?"

I shrugged, realizing I did not want to be having this conversation. I didn't want to revisit the horror that led to my discharge, nor regurgitate the sequence of events that left me here hiding behind three layers of clothing to mask the self-inflicted wounds on my left arm. I just wanted to check the necessary boxes off her list, and get approval to move on with my life.

"I can only imagine the darkness that is in that file." I asked.

"Yes," she answered.

I blinked, confused. It hadn't been a yes or no question. "Yes, what?" I pushed for her to explain.

"Darkness," she said softly.

Loneliness in a Crowd

As I drove home from Columbia, I thought about the content of my file, and the weight of my conscience. I looked over at the passenger seat at my rugged backpack that I now carried around with me everywhere. In some superficial way, it made me feel closer to Cameron, and I wasn't ready to put him down. I even buckled up the backpack in a safety belt, feeling a bit like a castaway with a volleyball named Wilson.

From inside the backpack, I heard a vibration…my cell phone was ringing. I unzipped the front pocket and pulled out my phone, keeping an eye on the road. On the other line was Angie's boyfriend, Brandon. He heard I was home and wanted to see me, and asked if I could meet him at the Alibi. Now *this* was more my kind of therapy.

Pulling into the once-familiar parking lot, however, I realized that I no longer felt home here. The owners had painted the exterior of the building and expanded their parking lot as business continued to thrive. Looking around and surveying the unfamiliar crowd in the room, apparently there were a lot of people who needed an alibi in this town. It used to be a little hole in the wall, a dive bar off the rural route toward Sierra's house. Now it had the appearance of a modern dance club, with neon lights in the windows.

Brandon greeted me in the parking lot, as soon as I stepped out of my car. "Welcome home, bro!" he said, attempting to come in for a bear hug. I reflexively stepped back and cautioned him to take it easy, reminding him of my shoulder. "Oh, yeah, I almost forgot about that!" he said. "Let's go inside and catch up on old times!"

He put his arm around me as we walked toward the front door. "A lot has changed since you've been here last. They totally renovated the whole place. Matter of fact, close your eyes…" He insisted that I keep my eyes closed as we walked through the front door. To be honest, I didn't care about any renovations. I preferred the familiar and traditional corner stool at the end of bar, and that's all I really wanted.

But I went along with his silly idea, and kept my eyes closed as he led me around the bar with his arm still around my shoulder. I could hear music on the jukebox, and a familiar song started as I walked in with my eyes still closed: "Born in the USA," by Bruce Springsteen. The irony was killing me.

"Okay, you can open your eyes now," Brandon said. I blinked my eyes and allowed them to adjust to... a room full of people staring at me in silence. All at once, they shouted in unison, "SURPRISE!" and a packed crowd began to cheer for me. "Welcome home, Jordan!" Angie shouted. Intermittent yelling and hugs, pats on the back from well wishers, and all around the bar, glasses were raised to the kid who never got a single vote for student council, who killed his best friend in the line of combat.

Suddenly, I was popular. As word had traveled around town, the reports of my heroism in recent combat (and the injury sustained from enemy fire) seemed to have created a fictitious account of actual events. I had become an overnight sensation to the local rumor mill, and the media campaigns seemed to idolize a man I knew didn't exist.

"What is this about?" I asked Brandon. I hadn't seen since most of the faces here since high school, and there were many people whom I had never even met. Brandon handed me a beer and said, "This is about you, man! It's about you fighting for our freedom, and taking shrapnel in your shoulder for a cause worth believing in!" Brandon raised his bottle in the air and shouted, "Let's raise a toast for our hometown John Rambo! Here's to Jordan Winter and the Purple Heart that kept him going in the hardest of times!"

It's extremely awkward to be the subject of unwanted and undeserved attention. Even if the intentions of those in the room were kind and pure, my conscience was unwilling to accept the accolades. After a round of applause, and as drinks were passed around the room, everyone's eyes and ears focused on me, clearly expecting me to make some kind of speech.

"Well, this was much unexpected, and I'm humbled by your reception. Thank you all for coming out tonight to greet me." As I looked around the room, I could sense that they wanted more. People wanted stories of bloodshed and fistfights and shootouts and exaggerated stories of excessive violence and bombs and Hollywood endings. But in that moment, all I could think of was, "The person y'all should be raising a toast to right now was just buried. Cameron is the real hero of this story. He paid the ultimate sacrifice, and he deserves to be here right now, not me."

After a few seconds of awkward silence, someone from the back of the room concurred. "Let's lift a glass to Cameron Bastian too!" The crowded room commenced to agreement, glasses and bottles clinked, and drinking ensued. I sat down on my familiar stool at the corner of the bar, and looked down at my watch, trying to calculate how quickly I could escape this scene without being noticed. It was all just too much, and my anxiety was starting to make me very, very thirsty.

"Hey, stranger! Do you remember me?" I turned to my left and focused my eyes on a beautiful girl in a short skirt, standing beside me. The whole room was spinning, and it was all so overwhelming… I stared blankly at her, but her name escaped me. I could feel my brain beginning to drown in the shallow end of a few too many drinks. She had a drink in her hand and hope in her eyes. I don't know how long I stood in awkward silence, my mind spinning like a computer searching for the answer to her question.

"Cassie," she said. "Sierra's friend… Remember, we shared a couch together one night, and you left the next morning without saying goodbye?" It all came back to me in that moment, and I suddenly regretted not being more social. She was beautiful, and all I could think about was how badly I wished I could have back that missed opportunity.

"I'm sorry, Cassie. Of course I remember you!" She leaned in to give me a hug and I could smell a hint of lavender and honeysuckle and all things holy. "I'm kind of an introvert. Please don't take it personally that I didn't talk to you more."

Cassie set her drink down on the bar and put her hand on my injured shoulder, tracing my sling softly with her fingers. She looked down for a minute, then looked up at me and said, "I'm just glad you're home safe, Jordan. Maybe we can revisit the couch sometime." She winked at me, and I took a step back, returning to the safety of my barstool. I suddenly had an urge to drink a gallon of bourbon and set something on fire. I was feeling the old familiar sting of anxiety, and yet I was craving the touch of a woman. The whole universe seemed to be calling my name at once, and the eyes of friends seemed to shine like stars. If only I could navigate my way home from the loneliness in a crowd of strangers.

My inward ache to discover love had become desensitized over the past few years. In as much as I wanted to find and be found in love, I was terrified at the vulnerability of being exposed. Perhaps I was overanalyzing Cassie's advancements toward me, but maybe my heart was occupied with a resident mystery. The truth would be found in the paradox of courage and fear, love and hate, grace and shame.

But whatever urge I had acquired to alleviate through alcohol, I buried deep under my newfound desire to be healthy. My recent commitment to God was sincere, and I could feel Him meeting me in my weakness. In the past, I would have drunk myself into an ocean of despair, but now I found the strength to walk away from the temptation. I retreated to the bathroom and locked the door. My cell phone battery was about to die. I opened my contacts and found Sierra, and sent her a quick text message. "Hey, you, is it okay if I stop by for a few minutes?" I hated texting, almost as much as I hated talking.

No response. I held my keys in my hand and contemplated

leaving without telling anyone. Maybe I could slip out the back door, or conjure up some excuse about a headache. I walked back out to the crowded room, where the music continued to blast through the speakers and the strangers mingled accordingly. While I had been in the bathroom, Cassie had begun a conversation with Angie. She stood at the bar with her jacket on, and it appeared she was about to make her exit too. I walked over to Brandon and apologized for interrupting his conversation. "Thanks for putting this together, man, but I need to get going. I've got a busy day tomorrow." He gave me a fist bump and nodded. "It's all good, man. Welcome home. Let's meet up here again soon, okay?"

As I was saying goodbye to Brandon, I saw Cassie waving at me from across the room as she walked toward the door. I waved in return, and watched her walk out. I wondered if she were upset with me for my nonverbal communication, or for not walking out with her. Looking back to face Brandon, I said, "I don't know, man, I'm trying to lay low for a while. But I'll be in touch."

By the time I got back on the road, it was getting late. The sun had set and the streetlights were flickering on. I still hadn't heard back from Sierra, but I figured since I was in the neighborhood, I'd swing by, so I took a left and drove down the back road that led to her farmhouse. I always loved the scenery surrounding her property. An open field separated the neighbor's barn from Sierra's garden. The garden had become overgrown, I noticed. As I slowed my car and pulled into the long driveway, I could see the fading paint that had begun to chip away in the winter wind. The front yard was also overgrown, and still covered in fallen leaves from last November. The bright light from her front porch revealed an empty swing, where I imagined Sierra was sitting when she first heard about Cameron's death.

I parked my car and walked up the driveway to the front porch. As I neared the door, I could hear the sound of an acoustic guitar playing, and the indiscernible lyrics of a feminine voice. I listened for a few minutes as Sierra played her guitar to a fussy baby. They were still learning a new normal, having been released from the hospital a few days earlier.

I knocked and waited. The strumming stopped, but the crying baby did not. From inside, I heard footsteps approaching the door as it eventually opened. Sierra stood before me in a faded t-shirt and pajama shorts. "Jordan!" she exclaimed. She reached out her hand and took me by the arm. "Come inside."

I followed Sierra into the living room, where a fireplace was emitting heat to sustain the entire house. Karis was wrapped in a blanket and intermittently crying in her crib. I stood over her and she looked up at me with instant confusion. She stopped crying and just stared at me. "Look at that!" Sierra laughed. "That's the first time she's stopped crying all night!" We just kept looking at each other, and neither the baby nor I moved. Sierra disappeared for a few moments and returned wearing a pair of sweatpants, I'm assuming to be more appropriate for her unexpected company.

She returned to pick up her guitar and began to softly strum. I did not take my eyes off Karis, but I spoke quietly to Sierra. "When did you learn how to play the guitar?" She continued to pick at the strings and said, "The day after I found out I was pregnant. I was going through a closet and found my grandpa's old guitar." She played a few notes and hummed a familiar tune. "I have no idea what I'm doing, but I've learned a few songs!" Sierra stood up next to me, overlooking Karis as she began to drift into a deep sleep. *"This little light of mine..."* She sang softly, *"I'm gonna let it shine..."*

I sat down on the couch and watched Sierra in all of her glory. No makeup, with messy hair and sweatpants, completely captivating. Sierra taught herself to play the guitar, because of course she did. And her first song to her infant daughter was about being a light that shines in the darkness, because of course she is.

I could have listened to her singing in that soft, earthy voice forever. Though she broke a string and sang off key, there was something authentic in her soulful voice. She even made up her own alternate verse. While continuing to repeat the chorus, Sierra sang, "And if the world caves in, I'm gonna let it shine..."

Her whole world had caved in around her, and she still had a song. She had loved and lost and found herself in the hurricane of confusion, a widow with an iron spine and a broken heart.

Shining, still.

Chapter 11

Extreme Home Makeover

A few months after my honorable discharge, I started receiving extended pay for the wounds I'd sustained in active combat. The Purple Heart award and Medal of Valor were external celebrations of an internal shame. But the financial support of the military allowed for me to put extra money away, and I chose to honor my commitment to Sierra by supporting her with the burden of continued medical costs for Karis' health condition.

I began to take an inventory of the various needs around her home, as Sierra pointed out her desire to sand and paint the outside of the house, as well as put up new roof shingles. I pulled out a massive ladder from her grandfather's barn, and leaned it against the side of the house. Climbing up the roof gave me a better visual of the surrounding acreage upon which the old farmhouse sat. It was a glorious sight. I sat down on the roof and made a list of duties that I was going to systematically perform for her. She was going to need new rain gutters, and the toilet needed a new flush chain. I needed to trim the hedges along the driveway, and address the invasive crabgrass growing in the front yard. And sometime in the next six months, I would be putting the last finishing touches on a brand-new roof for Sierra and Karis. My shoulder seemed to be healing well, but the muscles in my arms throbbed from daily workouts. As my left arm grew stronger, the scabs turned to scars. Eventually I was able to use both arms at full strength. I labored exhaustively at the mission of renovation, and spent hours wrestling with my memories.

Kneeling as I pounded nails into the shingles, Sierra kept me company. Somehow she managed to climb the ladder carrying a glass of sweet tea for me. She would wait until Karis was deep asleep in the afternoon heat before ascending the ladder and joining me.

"Tell me a story about Cam," she would say. And while I hammered away, I would spit out story after story that she had never heard before. He never bragged about himself, and if I had not witnessed his chivalry, I wouldn't have known these stories myself. I told her about my favorite memory: Cameron playing soccer with the Iraqi children, and the way he laughed with them in the eye of the hurricane. The casualties of war and the realities of evil had not contaminated the innocence of his heart.

"Tell me again about the time he told you I was pregnant!" she insisted. I set the hammer down and wiped the sweat from my brow. She handed me the glass of tea and I raised it in appreciation. After reminiscing on the story, I said, "I just remember he announced it in the prayer over our dinner. He kinda slipped it in there, subversively, to see if I caught it... and I did. That's when I told him I believed he was gonna be a great daddy."

Sierra looked out at the open field to the east. She watched a bird descend and land in the weeds, only to take off again within seconds. "Yes," she said wistfully. "He would have been an amazing father." However sad the stories made her, she always wanted to hear more. I told her about his reputation as a fearless leader, how he dismantled bombs and deescalated crisis. I shared with her about the ways he used to talk about her, and how he used to stare at her picture. "All he ever wanted was to get home to you," I said. She nodded slowly, lost in thought. "That's all I ever wanted, too."

Learning to Sing

I began to attend church with Sierra and Karis on a regular basis. The congregation was overwhelmingly supportive to them, and although I was truly happy they had such a tremendous support network, I was uncomfortable with all of the attention. Sierra was oblivious to the attention, and despite being a war widow, she manufactured a smile for the ages. She would sing along with the worship songs, and didn't even need to look at the words on the screen. I was distracted by the fact that she wasn't distracted. Instead of looking at the words on the screen, I just looked at her as she held Karis.

And every Sunday, without fail, Pastor Ryan seemed to pull on my heart strings with his sermons. He spoke with passion about the love of God and his infinite embrace. He read from the New Testament stories about Jesus and the way that he came to the defense of the guilty and showed forgiveness to those who were in need of salvation. I assumed that this was indeed good news for everyone—everyone, that is, except for me. Because I was pretty sure liars and thieves and murderers and drug addicts go to the lake of fire and burn forever in a bottomless pit called hell.

After church I would follow Sierra and Karis back to the house, and continue to whittle away at home renovations. One particular Sunday afternoon, the heat was unbearable. I had attempted to clear the field behind the house by collecting a brush pile, but the intensity of the sweltering September forced me to seek shade. I reluctantly walked back to the porch and took a seat on the swing. It was quiet inside the house, so I knew Karis had finally surrendered to her afternoon nap.

After a few minutes, Sierra stepped outside to join me on the porch. She was carrying a glass of her notorious sugar tea for me, and she took an obligatory sip before handing it over to me. "You need to stay hydrated, soldier." Sierra winked at me, and continued, "Unfortunately, it's not much cooler in the house than it is out here."

We sat on the porch and talked quietly for a short while, until silence prevailed. But it was a peaceful quiet, and we both seemed content to relax in each other's company. Sierra put her feet down and set the porch swing in motion; together, we rocked back and forth until she closed her eyes and leaned against my shoulder. At some point, Sierra fell asleep, while I continued swinging, and I remember feeling the inrush of a thousand volts of peace.

As she slept, I looked down at her delicate form. Her hair was a mess, and the spaghetti straps of her sundress had created a thin tan line on her shoulders. She had begun to develop smile wrinkles around her eyes, and even as they remained closed, I could get lost in the depths of her character. Her breathing was deep and heavy. I put my left arm around her, catching a glimpse of my arm, when I noticed my self-inflicted scars were fading. But my heart still had a long way to go.

The next Sunday at church, Pastor Ryan preached a sermon about love. He focused on the teaching of Jesus, who called his followers to "love your neighbor as your love yourself." It all looked good on paper, or in a warm, fuzzy theoretical devotion. But the more I thought about it, the more I wrestled with the application. I was distracted; as he continued to talk, I got lost in the question: *How can I love my neighbor if I hate myself?* It is possible to be so full of self-hatred that you can become incapable of truly loving others?

After the service, I waited in line to talk to Pastor Ryan. As Sierra went to get Karis from the church nursery, I thought about the challenging invitation of Jesus. Ever since that night in the abandoned parking lot, I had truly tried to understand the ways of God. But the deeper I buried my secret shame, the more difficult it became to feel any sense of a divine connection.

Pastor Ryan finished his conversation with an elderly woman

in front of me, and then turned to greet me. "Hey, Jordan, how are you?" I shook his hand and nodded, not sure if it was a greeting or a question. "I just wanted to ask you a question about the sermon this morning," I said. He sat down in the front row, motioning for me to join him. I sat down beside him, took a deep breath, and asked, "How can you truly love others if you hate yourself?"

The pastor looked concerned, uncertain as to what I meant. I was feeling nervous, but ever since I had stopped taking anti-anxiety medication, I was feeling much healthier. But now I wished I had a few Xanax to numb my discomfort. "I mean, the commandment is to love your neighbor as you love yourself, right? But what if you don't love yourself? In fact, what if you hate yourself?"

Pastor Ryan looked over my shoulder, pondering the question. He was often slow to speak, and I could tell that he was chewing on the dilemma. Fortunately, there was nobody else around, waiting to interrupt his train of thought. After what seemed like an eternity, he asked, "It's pretty heavy, isn't it?"

"What is?"

"That weight you're carrying around, Jordan... why do you hate yourself?"

"I can't tell you," I said, honestly. Just then I noticed Sierra had returned to look for me, carrying Karis in her arms. She slowly approached us in the front of the church, and Pastor Ryan smiled at her. Then turning back to me, he said, "It's one thing to forgive someone else. It's another thing to forgive yourself." After a brief pause, he added, "You might have left Baghdad, but the war has never left you."

Integers and Fractions

Over the course of time, I became increasingly comfortable opening up to Dr. Bailey. I was required to check in every Monday morning for a mandatory counseling session at the Warrior Transitional Unit in Columbia. However comfortable I felt talking to her, I never budged from my resolution to keep my shameful secrets hidden away behind a thousand locked doors. She had a way of knocking on those doors, however, and every now and then I would allow her to see my vulnerable side.

"How are things going with Sierra?" She asked. I added sugar to my coffee and stirred slowly. It was the kind of loaded question that I had come to expect from a therapist. I shrugged casually and nodded, the classic noncommittal answer. "Are you still working around the house and helping out with Karis?"

"Yes. I spend most of my afternoons clearing the field behind her house. Sierra wants to start a garden, but it's going to take a lot of work to cultivate the land. Sometimes she straps Karis on her back and comes out to talk with me while I work." As I sat back down on the couch, Dr. Bailey inquired, "Why?"

"Why, what?" I asked.

"Why are you so driven to work around the house for Sierra? What is driving this motivation?" Dr. Bailey asked, very directly. She was always searching for "the thing behind the thing," as if there were always an ulterior motive or questionable objective.

Outside the open window I could hear the sound of a lawnmower, and I could feel the warm, morning breeze circulating from the ceiling fan overhead. Dr. Bailey sat with her legs crossed, and I noticed a small tattoo of a rose on her ankle. My thoughts drifted back to the day I watched my dad get his tattoo, but she quickly brought me back to the conversation.

"I'm not sure what you're looking for," I answered. "I mean... she's a widow. She was married to my best friend. And it's the least I can do to honor Cam."

The pointed questions continued. "Are you developing feelings for her?"

"Feelings?" I echoed, and then snorted. "I can't remember the last time I had 'feelings' for anything. I think my 'feelings engine' was blown up somewhere back there in Iraq." I could tell that my answer seemed to concern Dr. Bailey, because she scribbled down some notes and made listening noises.

"You seem to compartmentalize a lot of important things in your life, Jordan," she said quietly. "It's almost as if you keep your feelings locked up in one room, and your actions in another room. Your emotions are distinctly absent from your thoughts. For example, you seem to care very much about Sierra, but you don't allow yourself to show it."

I didn't respond. I just fidgeted in my seat and looked around for a clock to count down the minutes until I could leave. Going to these weekly counseling sessions had begun to feel like weekly trips to the dentist. I just wanted the conversation to be over. But it wasn't.

"Are you familiar with the concept of an integer?" Dr. Bailey asked. Taking me back to elementary school mathematics, she said, "An integer is a whole number. It's not a fraction, and it's not divided. One, two, three, four... never is it five and one-half." I shrugged again, and nodded, wondering where she was going with all of this mathematical jargon. "An integer is the same root word for where we get the idea of 'integrity,'" Dr. Bailey concluded. "And you need to start healing the fractions inside your heart so you can become a man of integrity."

Falling Forward

That evening, as I was burning the last of the brush pile, I heard Sierra call out from the kitchen window, "Dinner's ready!" She closed the window quickly, and I looked up at the ominous sky, as dark clouds seemed to gather quickly. The summer heat lightening had begun to flash, and by the time I put out the last of the flames, the rain began to drop like stars from the sky. I walked quickly toward the house, but not before my shirt was soaked in the sudden downfall.

Stepping inside quickly, I took off my muddy boots at the door. "That rain came out of nowhere!" I said. Sierra was feeding Karis with a tiny spoon in the kitchen. She looked over toward me and said, "Stay right there, you're filthy!"

She disappeared into the back bedroom and said, "Take your shirt off too. I'm doing a load of laundry tonight. I'll throw your stuff in." After a minute, she walked out to meet me as I had remained standing in the doorway. "Here," she said, "Put this on." She handed me one of Cam's old t-shirts. I held it and looked at her, unsure.

"Go on," she said. "You can't stay in those soaking wet clothes!" With that, she turned on her heel and walked back to resume feeding Karis in the kitchen. I stripped my wet shirt off, and replaced it with the clean shirt last worn by her late husband. It fit perfectly, and it still smelled like Cam. I walked into the kitchen and sat down at the table, where a. plate of chicken, biscuits, and gravy was waiting for me. "Thank you, Sierra," I said. "You sure know the way to a man's heart."

After dinner, Sierra gave Karis a bath and I washed the dishes. She attempted to lay her down in the crib for the night, but I could hear Karis screaming in resistance. After I dried the dishes and put them away, I folded the towel and walked down the hallway to the baby's room. Sierra was frustrated, and I could tell that she was exhausted. I slowly walked over to the crib and stood next to Sierra as she tried to console her baby girl. I didn't say anything at first, but I slowly reached down and began to rub her back. Karis looked up at me and stopped crying for a few seconds, before resuming her infant insurrection. I put both of my hands out and picked her up, pulling her close to me. Immediately, Karis stopped crying.

Sierra rolled her eyes and smiled. She walked out to turn off the hallway light, and I carried Karis over to the rocking chair in the corner of her bedroom. A small lamp flashed stars on the ceiling, and I whispered and shushed and wooed her to join me in the observation of the cosmic wonder of it all.

I whispered softly in her ear, as Karis rested against my chest. I told her stories about Billy the Bear and Timmy the Turtle. I made up fictional portrayals of a princess in a land far, far away. After a while, I glanced down and noticed Karis had fallen into a deep sleep.

And then I noticed Sierra.

She had been standing in the doorway for what must have been quite some time. She was watching me, as I held Karis. I don't know how long she was standing there, but it must have been a while, because she seemed lost in her thoughts. I slowly stood and walked Karis back over to her crib, placing her gently down for the night. I turned off the lamp, and turned to face Sierra. She was standing in the doorway, and as I turned to walk out, she did not move. I stood before her, wondering if she was trying to whisper something to me. She leaned in, as if to tell me a secret...

Sierra kissed me, softly. She put her hands around the back of my head and pulled me closer. She kissed me like her life depended on it. Deeply, thoroughly, with all of her delicate heart, Sierra launched herself into me like a sea boat captain jumping from a sinking ship. And just like that, the engine of my feelings had been resurrected from the ashes.

I loved Sierra. God knows I've always loved her. I have loved her from a distance and I have loved her from as close as a kiss. I have loved her as a sister and I have loved her as a friend. Still, in this present moment, I was caught in the tension of loving my neighbor while hating myself.

As we stood in the doorway of Karis's bedroom, I held Sierra in my arms, and together we became lost in the moment; an epiphany of being sealed by love and the inevitable climax of regret and hope and wonder and yes.

Chapter 12

All Is Fair (In Love and War)

Over the next few years, I lost and found myself in the familiar chorus of "Amazing Grace." The echoes of a world still at war seemed to be silenced in the comfort of Sierra's embrace. She had a way with words, and she had a way with silence. She could finish my sentences and silence my worries. Sierra melted my frozen heart with her fingertips on fire, and her kisses became my permanent address. It had been over four years since Cameron had died, and Sierra seemed ready to move forward with her life.

She taught me how to dance. At the end of every week, she insisted that we enjoy our "Saturdates." She'd clear out the living room furniture to create an open floor for slow dancing. I let her lead, and begged her not to tell anyone. She would put on a mixed compilation of her favorite love songs, and together we would spin and twirl and laugh and climb and fall and start all over again.

Sierra had a way of reading my mind. It was as if she could look into my eyes and see my tormented soul, and although she was concerned for my well-being, she never pried loose anything I wasn't ready to share. And the grip around my secret shame was still securely sealed with white knuckles and trembling hands.

A year after my honorable discharge, I successfully completed my counseling sessions with Dr. Bailey, and successfully managed to keep my secret hidden away. Although many of the sessions attempted to unlock the trauma associated with violence and regret, I never allowed the reflections to become transparent enough to incriminate me. I had become an artist at vague confessions, because being vague was like camouflage—my favorite color.

The Army still sent me a residual paycheck every month as a way of "honoring my valor." The accumulated savings from active combat pay, combined with my part-time hours at the lumberyard, afforded me the luxury of a nice apartment on the north side of Charleston.

The presence of my mother in our shared apartment was very comforting. We were able to rebuild trust, and talked openly about our feelings. From the moment I brought her home from the abusive relationship in the mobile home, she seemed to be at peace.

Although I spent most of my free time with Sierra and Karis, my mom did her best to make the apartment feel more like a home. There were many nights when we she would linger over a pot of homemade chili, waiting for me to come home for dinner. By the time I arrived, she had been sitting alone for hours, and I would apologize profusely.

"Tell me about Sierra," she would say. "How is she?"

This was the typical, late night conversation my mother and I would have as I sat at the kitchen table, devouring her neglected cooking. "She's amazing," I would say. We also talked about Karis and her endless laughter. I loved that little girl like she was my own. I carried pictures of her around in my wallet, and showed them off to anyone who expressed even an ounce of interest.

I loved Karis because she first loved me. She relentlessly pursued my affections. From the time she could take her first steps to the time I taught her how to balance on her bicycle, Karis chased me down with her tender heart. She insisted on holding my hand everywhere we went, and was always within my eyesight.

She tore down the concrete walls around my heart with the innocent violence of her love. Before I could realize it, she had unassumingly dismantled my shame, allowing me to love and be loved. And as Sierra watched from a mother's distance, Karis taught me how to live again.

Hide and Seek

Sierra and I shared a deep and beautiful friendship, but we were so much more. We were truly in love with each other, and over the next few years, we talked about marriage and the "happily ever after." I began to save up for an engagement ring, and together we dreamed of moving closer to the beach. And although her tender disposition never changed, over the years Sierra seemed less interested in throwing house parties. She was more content to devote her intimate energy toward being a mother, and didn't seem to care about much else, except me, of course.

I would drive over to Sierra's house on Sunday mornings, and the three of us would pile into my Jeep. Our Sunday ritual included stops for coffee and donuts on the way to church, and then ice cream on the way home. Sometimes my mother would join us, but she preferred to attend the Presbyterian Church with Aunt Tracy.

I remember one evening in late October, and the time change robbed us of an hour's daylight. As Sierra scurried around the kitchen preparing dinner, I agreed to play in a game of hide-and-seek with Karis. This was, by far, her favorite way to spend time with me. Squealing with excitement, she ran from the kitchen into the living room, shouting at the top of her lungs, "Come and try to find me!" I counted obnoxiously loud, all the way to thirty. "Ready or not, here I come!" Sierra giggled, "Take it easy on her, Jordan!" Taking four steps from the kitchen into the living room, I saw an adorable lump (about the size of a four-year-old girl) trembling under a blanket in the center of the floor. Seriously? I mean, couldn't she at least move to the corner?

Because Karis is grace, and grace doesn't hide very well. It is exposed at every corner, laughing and anxious to be discovered. Grace is more interested in being found than staying hidden. It is like the rising sun, screaming for attention.

"Sierra!" I yelled, "I have no idea where Karis is hiding. Can you help me?" She walked into the room trying hard to conceal her laughter, winking, "Jordan... where did she go?" The mysterious lump under the blanket began to shake with the sound of mischievous laughter and a child shrieking, "I'm in the wiving woom!"

Sierra whispered to me, "Could she possibly be any cuter?" And in that instant, I collapsed onto the floor next to Karis and pulled back her blanket, tickling her to the point of near torture. She laughed so hard that she farted, which made her laugh even more.

But now, she insisted, it was my turn to hide.

She put her hands over her eyes and buried her face in the couch as she counted, "One, two, three..." I bolted up the stairs, instinctively. Down the hallway, I tiptoed into the guest bedroom and continued to scramble instinctively into the darkness of unfamiliar territory. I opened the window and climbed out, scaling the exterior of the second floor of the old farmhouse until I pulled myself to the rooftop. I crawled along the shingles all the way to the chimney, where I curled up to hide in the shadows. I looked up at the moon, and the threatening clouds.

Shame hides like a tree in a forest. It is the impulsive reflex of a darkness running from the light. After prolonged self-hatred, shame finds comfort under layers of scar tissue, where resentment is born.

My thoughts drifted back to the addiction, the attempted intervention, and the smell of gunfire. After a short while, I was brought back to the present moment when I heard Sierra calling my name. She was probably wondering where I was.

Post-Traumatic Stress Disorder

There was a thunderous knock at my front door. I could hear yelling and the ominous sound of a helicopter or a chainsaw or an engine running violently, drowning out the screams. Blue lights flashing, a siren in the distance, and I did not know if they were friends or enemies. I reached for my handgun beside the bed, and I checked the chamber. No bullets. I began to search the top drawer frantically for ammunition, as the pounding at the front door continued... they were coming for me, and I was not going down without a fight.

Without bullets, my gun was pointless. I ran to the closet to look for a weapon with which to defend myself, but as I opened the closet door, I was shocked to find completely empty shelves... I could hear the sound of gunfire outside, and I ducked from the window and it was too late, I had been hit! I gasped for air, feeling the suffocation of an uncertain enemy.

But just then, I lunged forward in my sleep, awoken from a violent nightmare. Breathing heavy and sweating profusely, I stared up at the ceiling fan circling above us as Sierra was disturbed. We had fallen asleep on the couch in the living room, with the television still blaring in the background. She sat up and looked at me, "Jordan?"

I wiped the sweat from my forehead and looked at the clock. It was just after midnight, and I was having another flashback. The dreams had become so disturbing that I hated to sleep alone, and Sierra would often let me sleep on the couch with her. "Are you okay?" She asked. But she knew I was very much not okay. I was falling apart.

She got up from the couch and went into the kitchen, returning with a cup of water. I took it from her and chugged every last drop. "So, are you going to tell me what happened in the dream?" she wondered.

I shook my head and said, "I don't want to talk about it. You know that." I stood up and grabbed my jacket as if to leave. She pulled my sleeve toward her. "Come here," she said.

"Don't leave." I sat back down on the couch and looked at her, never minding the gravitational forces that yanked a solo tear from my eye.

Together, we sat. We were not uncomfortable in our silence, and somehow it all seemed to make sense: Nonverbal communication, emotional healing in the affirmation of presence. She had a way of chasing away the bad dreams, with the interlocking fingers that reminded me that her light is always left on for me.

A few days later, Sierra convinced me to schedule an appointment with Dr. Bailey. She insisted that I seek out someone to talk with, and to be honest about the nightmares. "Would it help if I joined you?" she asked. "I mean...I might be able to add a new perspective." I thought about the irony of feeling safe with Sierra, yet the tyranny of hesitation that kept me from opening up about the truth of what happened that fateful day in Baghdad. I wanted to protect her from the heartache and anguish of knowing what really happened. Or perhaps I just wanted to manipulate the situation so that she wouldn't hate me any more than I already hated myself.

"Yes," I said. "I think it would be helpful if you joined me." But I knew that I could never fully open up about the details. Sierra looked up the number to the office in Columbia, then she handed me the phone to schedule the appointment. Four days later we were sitting side by side on a couch, like a scene from a movie.

Dr. Bailey greeted Sierra casually, as I blew steam from my coffee cup. "I'm so glad you were able to join us today, Sierra," she said. "I'm glad to finally meet you. Jordan has told me a lot about you, and I think your insights will be invaluable." Sierra had never been in a psychiatrist's office before, yet she seemed confident in her demeanor. I looked over at her as she began talking with Dr. Bailey. I noticed her hair was tucked back behind her ear, and all I wanted in that moment was to capture it in a picture, so I blinked hard and downloaded the epic cuteness into my memory bank.

The session started off rather slowly, but eventually landed on the central theme of my coping with the aftermath of a traumatic series of events. Dr. Bailey focused her questions to Sierra, hoping to understand how deep my potential diagnosis had grown. "What does it look like when Jordan gets angry?" she asked. "Does he raise his voice or threaten violence?"

Sierra shook her head. "No. Never."

Dr. Bailey continued with the questions. "And is he gentle with your daughter?"

"Of course. He's amazing with her!" Sierra answered. "He's the only daddy she's ever known. She likes to chase him around, and they like to play games. The other night, he read her a story and she fell asleep right on his lap." Sierra reached over and took my hand. Then she continued, "But my main concern is the intensity of his nightmares."

Dr. Bailey turned her attention toward me. "Can you tell me about the dreams, Jordan?" I felt Sierra's grip tighten in my hand.

"It's hard to remember the details," I said. "But it's usually some sort of violent episode. A fight, maybe, or a chase. And there's usually a reason for frustration, like my car won't start or there is too much smoke to see the enemy. And sometimes I have a dream I'm being shot at, but I don't know where to hide for cover."

Dr. Bailey nodded and scribbled notes while I continued. "The other night I had a dream they were about to break through the front door and get me."

"Who are 'they'?" Dr. Bailey inquired.

It was a good question. I had no idea who the enemy was, exactly. Not anymore. "The bad guys," I said, after a moment's pause. "Or maybe it's the good guys, and I'm the antagonist in my own story." Sierra shook her head, offering emotional support. Dr. Bailey continued writing in her notebook even after I had stopped talking. Sierra broke the silence. "He wakes up sweating profusely, and usually can't go back to sleep. I am quite worried about his emotional exhaustion and mental health."

Dr. Bailey looked up from notes and looked directly at me. She spoke with confidence, and it was comforting to be in the circumference of certainty. "What you're describing are symptoms often associated with Post-Traumatic Stress Disorder. Not to minimize the diagnosis, but this sounds like a classic case of survivor's guilt and the brain's ongoing efforts to make sense of a compound disturbance."

I had heard these terms thrown around before, especially in the last few years. But it wasn't until this moment that I realized I was very mentally and emotionally wounded. Dr. Bailey continued, "It's almost like a bomb detonated inside your own brain, decimating your cognitive wires." I nodded slowly, as things began to make sense.

Dr. Bailey turned a few pages back in her notepad and pointed out a comment. "In one of our initial conversations, I asked you to recall when Cameron was killed. Do you remember what you told me?"

I scratched my head and couldn't seem to recall the conversation. Sierra looked at me and then turned to Dr. Bailey. "What did he say?" I echoed her question. "Yeah, what did I say?"

Dr. Bailey read directly from her notes. "You said, 'it was all a blur'." Somewhat relieved that I hadn't said too much, I mumbled, "That's pretty accurate." My dreams (as well as my memories) seemed to be a hazy fog of confusion. I could remember certain insignificant details, but other times I could hardly remember my own name.

Sierra leaned over and put her head against my shoulder. She asked, "Is there anything we can do to unlock the memories, or heal the PTSD?" I put my arm around her, and rubbed her back as Dr. Bailey suggested a few daily treatment exercises.

"Your inability to express yourself verbally does not seem consistent with your psychological test results. Jordan, you have an extremely high IQ score, and your level of self-awareness is off the charts." Sierra looked at me as I picked anxiously at my cuticles, causing the skin beneath my fingernail to bleed. Dr. Bailey continued, "I highly recommend you begin writing in a journal a few times a week, just recording your thoughts and daily activities. We can revisit some of your entries in our next session. But at the core of what we're hoping for is you can practice the art of being *fully present*. Do you know what I mean by that?"

I shrugged, assuming that it sounded self-explanatory. But Dr. Bailey explained, "You are in pursuit of wholeness and integrity, Jordan. Remember when we talked about that? We get the idea of integrity from the root word, 'integer,' which is a whole number. It is not a fraction, nor is it divided." She continued, "There is a chance that some of your memories, and nightmares, could have something to do with the 'fractures' you're feeling on the inside. One way you can reclaim your sense of self or identity is by learning new self-disciplines, and challenging yourself to be focused with your mental and emotional energy. If this all sounds like gibberish, just ask yourself the question, 'When's the last time I was able to listen to Karis tell me a story without being distracted by a mental checklist of other things?'"

That counseling session would be a turning point in my life. I knew that I had become divided over time, holding on to grace and shame in the same breath. I knew that I had left the war, but the war had never left me. I knew that I was unsure of where I belonged, and that 'home' was an abstract idea that I could not get my head around. I was present but I was absent. I was fighting, but I was hiding. I was running, but I was standing still.

Chapter 13

Declaration of Dependence

My heart had become searched, seized, and sealed by Sierra. I loved her with a reckless intentionality. I loved the way she whispered my name to wake me from the nightmares. I loved the way her hair began to curl around her shoulders, and cascaded down the small of her back. I loved her bare feet (and the curious case of her perpetual cleanliness), and the luscious shades of purple polish. I loved the way she would sing along with the radio, even though we both knew she didn't know the words... she would make them up. I loved the way she used to dance with Karis in the living room. "There's only one thing to do in this situation," she would say. "Turn up the music!"

I had arrived on the inevitable conclusion she loved me, although I wasn't sure how or why. I did not find myself very lovable. Maybe that was because I knew the disgusting truths about myself that nobody else knew. Perhaps, I thought, if she really knew the truth, she wouldn't love me. Therefore, she loved a version of me, but not the whole of me, because the whole of "me" was an ass.

But I tried to love her as best I could. I remained committed to earning my forgiveness, working to find redemption through manual labor. I worked relentlessly around Sierra's house, putting up drywall in Karis' bedroom, and finishing the development of a fourth bedroom Sierra wanted to convert to a guest bedroom. With every swing of the hammer, I imagined myself one strike closer to the finish line. I hoped that Cameron would have been pleased, and that somehow I could finally make him proud. I wondered if he were somewhere in the afterlife, watching me. Had he forgiven me? How could he, if I hadn't even forgiven myself?

One night, Sierra and I took Karis out for ice cream and a walk through the park. It was the Sunday following the Daylight Savings, and everyone seemed to be in a good mood. Charleston is beautiful in the spring, and the tall palm trees swayed gently in the ocean breeze. Karis walked between us, holding each of our hands. I couldn't believe how big she was getting. Sierra was talking about putting her in kindergarten this September.

While we were walking, we heard someone call out for Sierra. She turned and saw Cameron's parents walking with some of their friends. "Hey, there! We thought that was you." Cameron's mother greeted Sierra with a warm hug, and bent down to kiss her granddaughter on the forehead. "Look at this little girl, getting so big!" Sierra had established a monthly rhythm of bringing Karis to visit her grandparents on the first Saturday of each month. They had maintained a good relationship, and focused their conversations on Karis' activities and health.

Cameron's father Jim, reached out to shake my hand.

"Jordan," he said, "It's good to see you. How are you doing?" I returned the handshake, nodding. "I'm doing well, sir. Very blessed by good friends." I looked over at Karis as she entertained a small group of admirers with her new set of gymnastic tricks. While Sierra talked to them, I continued a private conversation with Jim Bastian. The truth is, once Sierra and I made the transition from friends to lovers, I had not seen much of them. Perhaps they were avoiding me… or maybe it was the other way around. The awkwardness was disconcerting, however kind Cameron's parents remained.

"What have you been up to? What are you doing for work these days?" he asked. I had not held down full-time employment since my discharge, spending most of my time working to upgrade Sierra's farmhouse. "Honestly, I've been working hard on renovating Sierra's house. I haven't been working on much else." I swatted at a pestering mosquito before continuing. "And I'm still working part-time at the lumber mill, and I'm using that income to help take care of my mom, who's been living with me."

As Sierra and Karis wandered over to join our conversation, Cam's father invited us to their home for their annual Fourth of July party. "We usually have the whole neighborhood show up just in time to watch the fireworks from our backyard. We'd be thrilled to have y'all over this year!" I picked up Karis and nodded. "I'm sure these girls would love it. I am not sure if I'd be up for it, but I certainly appreciate the invite."

The truth is I would rather eat glass than attend that party. Just the idea of crowd full of rednecks lighting off fireworks and patting me on the back for my Medal of Valor made me want to vomit.

As we turned to leave, Cameron's mother, Pamela, said, "You know, I just thought of this… Jordan, why don't you join us for the Independence Day Parade this year? Everyone would love to see you, and it would be a great opportunity to wear your uniform again and show everyone your Purple Heart!"

Ugh. I'd rather drink acid.

But I nodded politely, and waved as we turned to walk away. The inrush of memories came flooding back, and seeing the Bastian family made me miss Cameron in a way that I didn't know I possibly could. I missed him like a person craves water in a desert, aching for a return to the innocence. I missed the way Cam used to see through my hardened front, and know the true me. He was probably the only person who truly knew me and loved me anyway.

The unexpected reunion with Cameron's parents triggered feelings of profound sadness for both Sierra and me. We didn't discuss it, but as we walked away, she was quiet. I looked over at her and she seemed lost in a faraway land. Even as Karis continued to talk endlessly, Sierra looked off into the distance. I had seen that 'thousand-yard stare' in the eyes of men returning from war, and I wondered if she had her own trauma that had gone undiagnosed but nonetheless undisputed. She missed Cameron too, and seeing his parents reopened the wounds she had been trying to heal.

For the next several days, I worked with a focused determination to finish the trenches, digging the underground sprinkling lines around her property. Dig, toss, sweat, repeat. My hands were blistered and calloused from the wooden shovel, and my back was blistered from the early summer sun. I worked from dawn's first light, until the evening shadows no longer permitted me to see. And all the while, Sierra sat motionless on the porch, looking off into the setting sun.

I knew something was wrong, but I couldn't find the words. Maybe she hadn't fully healed from the nuclear loss of her first love. Maybe we had moved too quickly into a romantic relationship, and her heart wasn't ready. Maybe she was vulnerable and I was taking advantage of her loneliness. Maybe she was reconsidering her feelings for me. Maybe she wanted to be left alone, thank you very much. Maybe there is no amount of yard work I could do to bring Cameron back to us. Maybe redemption looked like an open door and burning candle and a front porch swing, and maybe there is no forgiveness for the prodigal son of a prodigal son.

Days turned into weeks, and the distance remained. The silence was not intended to have been cruel, but we worked our way around each other, trembling and bleeding from interior blisters. No matter the silence around the house, Karis followed me around the yard as I worked. She took peculiar interest in my calloused hands, even as the shovels and the dirt hid the wounds. Karis would run back to the house and return to me carrying a tiny fistful of Band-Aids. "You have ouches on your hands," she whispered. I set down my shovel and she held out the bandages. "Let me see."

I held out my hands to hers. She looked at them with ferocious intensity, and then looked up at me. She didn't say anything, just kept shaking her head incredulously. Then she reached up and kissed my bleeding hands. Her beautiful, innocent face was now smeared with my blood and dirt and shame.

Karis turned and ran back into the house, leaving me standing paralyzed outside. My wounded heart was being renovated by her tender insistence that I was loved. And yet every time I saw her, I thought, *I'm the reason you don't have a daddy.* But one time Sierra told me that every time Karis saw me, she thought *if it weren't for you, I wouldn't have a daddy.* And there was nothing I could ever do to make her love me any more, or any less, than the infinite supply she already held for me.

Just as I turned back to resume digging, Karis came walking down the porch carrying a glass of ice water for me. Because, of course she was.

Rock Bottom (Has a Hole in the Basement Floor)

By the first week of July, I had managed to finish most of the underground sprinkling labor, and Sierra's grass began to glisten in the appreciation of endless water. The timed frequencies allowed for Sierra to monitor her beautiful landscape without lifting a finger. She was grateful to see the deep shades of green emerge beneath the shade trees in her front yard, and she began to spend her mornings weeding the garden beside her house.

On the morning of Independence Day, I slept in later than usual. My mother had cooked a full breakfast, but it was cold by the time I walked out to the kitchen to join her. She was sitting at the table, reading the newspaper. "Good morning, Jordan. I made coffee about an hour ago. Do you want some?" I sat down at the table and nodded gratefully.

"Are you going to be joining us today?" my mother asked casually. She poured a cup of coffee, and handed it to me. I was still waking up, confused. "Who is 'we,' and what are your plans?" I cautiously asked. She apologized, "Oh, I'm sorry. I thought you knew... A bunch of us are going to the town parade and then to the Bastians' party this evening. Sierra invited me, and I figured you were coming."

This was definitely not something I was aware of, and I had no interest in going. I stood up from the kitchen table and walked over to the window, looking out. It was late morning, and the sky was laced in a cryptic shade of blue. A few scattered clouds created shadows on the landscape outside, and as I thought about Sierra going to Cameron's parents' house for the evening, I had an unsettling sadness. Perhaps I was jealous, or insecure. Or maybe I was just still running from the truth.

"No," I said. "I'm not going to be joining you." I went back to my room and reemerged a few minutes later with a pair of beach shorts and a tank top. "Have you seen my backpack, Mom?" I asked. She looked up from the newspaper and smiled. "Are you going to the beach? That's a good idea! It's beautiful outside." My mother stood up from the kitchen table and walked over to the closet, pulling out my old backpack. "Who are you going with?"

"I'm going alone," I said. "And please don't put my bag in the closet. I need it." As I turned to leave, my mom asked, "Why do you always carry that bag around with you?" I didn't answer because I didn't know. It just felt like home. I wasn't even sure what was still in there; probably the same old trash I'd had since Baghdad. But somehow, it felt good around my shoulders, and I felt naked without it.

By the time I got to the beach, it was almost noon. It was nearly impossible to find parking because of the holiday, and although I'd been hoping to spend some time in solitude, it seemed impossible. What was once a sacred refuge had been overrun from tourists and transplants. I ignored the No Parking signs, joining the countless other vehicles lined up illegally. I parked near Whitey's Surf Shop and walked directly toward the water.

Charleston in July is an oven. The sand immediately burned my bare feet, so I stopped and threw on a pair of flip-flops. In the distance I could see the gentle blue water and the soft breaking waves. I immediately regretted not having brought my surfboard, but the waves were probably too small to ride anyway. I couldn't remember the last time I had surfed... it must have been with Cam and Sierra shortly after we graduated from high school. The water lapped at my scalding feet, and I felt the relief of the Atlantic Ocean. As I walked along the shore, children chased the receding waves. On any other day I wouldn't have minded, but today I was feeling a tsunami of sadness.

Although I had tried to rebuild my life from the ashes of regret, the shame was catching up with me. I wondered if it were too late to come clean, and whether the ramifications would land me in prison. I thought about my dad, and determined that the possible consequences outweighed the benefits. After all, what good would it bring for the people I loved? It wouldn't bring Cameron back to us. It would reopen the scabs forming scar tissue in a thousand broken hearts. The idea of puking up a confession seemed self-serving, like I was getting things off my chest. But the pain would just be transmitted to the people around me, and it would only make things worse. So I resolved to keep rolling the dice. I didn't want to lose Sierra and Karis.

I must have walked along the beach for a few hours. After a while, my backpack started to feel heavy on my shoulder, but I was so caught up in my hurricane of emotions that I didn't notice. No matter how far I walked, the crowds remained. Once I stopped to sit down, I honestly had no idea where I was, or how far I'd wandered. I sat down in the sand and looked up at the sky, until I couldn't keep my eyes open anymore.

I've Been Up To No Good

Someone was pounding on the door. A man was screaming at me to open up, but I didn't recognize the voice. The pounding increased, someone started ringing my doorbell, and dogs started howling. I tried to peek out the window to get a glimpse of who was at the door, but it was all blurry. Who's there?" I tried to shout, but the words wouldn't come out. I was trying to get dressed, but I couldn't find my clothes anywhere.

Suddenly the door exploded open and all I could hear was screaming, sirens, and the sound of gunshots, practically blinded by the glare of blue lights. I tried to cover up, but it was too late. I was hit, spinning, and losing my breath. Gasping and coughing, I sat up quickly, awoken from another nightmare.

I must have fallen asleep on the beach. By now it was early evening. The beach crowds had dissipated, and now I was finally alone. As I lay back down, I looked up at the sky, now covered with clouds. My hair clung to my forehand in a sweaty mop, and my arms were sunburned. I wondered if my blood pressure was high, or if the bad dream had unleashed chemical warfare in my system. By now, I was agitated and depressed, and for the first time in a long time, suicidal.

For years I had been living with the guilt of my conscience, but I had learned to adjust, as if to walk with a spiritual limp. But the shame had begun to eat away at my peace, like a cancer that slowly invaded my heart. The thought of Sierra lighting fireworks in the backyard of Cam's parents' house had fueled a deep resentment within me. I had been living a lie, and in the sweltering heat of this Independence Day, I was letting go.

As I leaned back against my backpack, I realized I'd lost track of time. I took my cell phone out of my backpack and saw I had four missed calls from Sierra, along with one short voicemail:

"Hey, Jordan, I'm just trying to get a hold of you. Karis and I are going to head over to the party at Cam's parents' house. Are you coming with us? I haven't heard from you all day, and I'm beginning to worry about you. Please call me."

The lack of reception at the beach had exhausted my phone's battery, which was constantly searching for a signal. Just as I tried to dial Sierra's number, my phone began to shut down. Maybe that was for the best, because I didn't know what I was planning to say anyway. But one thing was clear: I was not up for a social event at the home of the parents whose son I had killed.

I threw my phone back into my backpack, and decided to finally peruse through whatever I had shoved away over the years. I pulled out my old journal and a few pictures taken from basic training. Rereading some of the entries brought me back to the diversity of emotions that accompanied me from my first day in Baghdad until the day of my "honorable discharge."

Turning to the last page of the journal, I pulled out a pen and wrote these words:

i don't want to live like this
i'd rather die

i want to swim with the sharks
and run with the bulls
i want to jump from a bridge
that separates me from you

i want to cut my wrists into a thousand miles of
hypocritical pain

> and take a chainsaw to the mirror with a hush and
> whisper and fist
>
> i am suffocating on the inside
> and breathing secondhand smoke for dear life

I poured out the rest of the contents from my backpack onto the sand. Out tumbled an old t-shirt, socks, a belt, a devotional book that Chaplain Acheson once gave me, an unsent letter to my father, a copy of *War and Peace*, and small container filled with prescription pills. The label had faded and I could not read the words, but I assumed it was probably painkillers, or maybe Xanax.

I threw everything back into the backpack and began the arduous journey back toward my car. The sun was beginning to lower in the western horizon, and eventually disappeared beyond the palm trees scattered along Folly Beach Boulevard.

Once I finally made it back to Whitey's Surf Shop, my car was gone. It must have gotten towed for parking illegally, and to make matters worse, my cell phone was dead. By this time, my temper was escalating to a scary place. I was so angry I just started to walk back toward town, and realized that it was probably better that I wasn't around anyone anyway.

I had a $20 bill in my front pocket, and walked across the street to the liquor store. I headed straight for the counter and pointed to the Absolut Vodka behind the cashier. All I wanted was to escape from the pain of a torturous existence.

"Jordan?"

I turned to face the voice behind me. It was my old drinking buddy, Brandon. I hadn't seen him since the surprise party that he threw for me at The Alibi. "Hey, man," I said quietly. He walked up and stood beside me at the counter, refusing to let me pay. Brandon handed the cashier his credit card and said, "Let me get this. Put it on my card."

I started to protest, but Brandon threw his arm around me and said, "It's the Fourth of July, and I'm gonna get lit with my favorite soldier!" The cashier handed me the vodka, and we walked outside. "Here's the deal, man…" I said. "I'm not in the mood to socialize. I am not a war hero. I am not who you think I am. I appreciate your kindness, but I really just want to be alone."

Brandon pulled out a cigarette and lit it. He nodded as he inhaled. "Yeah, man, I get it. The Fourth of July probably brings flashbacks of all the bombs and stuff. No worries, bro." I didn't say anything, but I opened the bottle and took my first drink in a long time. I felt the smoldering fire of pure vodka burning me from the inside out.

"Are you driving?" Brandon asked. He looked around for my car as I took another drink. "My car got towed. Can you believe that mess?" I said. Brandon pointed to his truck in the parking lot. "I'm headed to The Alibi to meet up with some friends. Get in— I'll give you a ride back that way at least."

Considering my options, it seemed fitting. I climbed into the passenger seat without saying a word. Brandon drove in silence, letting the radio alleviate the otherwise awkward silence. I didn't care about anything anymore. I drank hard, right from the bottle, and fast. And the fact that I hadn't eaten anything all day probably sped up the initial buzz. I wanted to smash and get smashed. I wanted to pass out and wake up forgetting my whole existence.

By the time we pulled into the parking lot, my vision had begun to blur. A large group was sitting outside on the patio deck as he got out of the car. He walked over to the passenger side and opened the door for me to get out.

Everyone saw me getting out of Brandon's truck, and it had been a long time since I'd shown my face. Considering the southern patriotism on Independence Day, it was only fitting that I would show up to bar with old-school friends. Immediately, people began to call my name. I didn't exactly want to be around anyone, but I was already beginning to feel the loss of inhibitions. I carried the vodka with me into the bar, and within five minutes I had three more beers brought to my table. "This is on the house!" Angie gave me a hug, and welcomed me back to my old stomping grounds. "Sometimes you just have to go where everybody knows your name. Cheers!"

There I sat, surrounded by nameless faces and the white noise of a hero's welcome. The kind intentions of these acquaintances only served to swallow me into the blackness of self-hatred. I was not a war hero. They were celebrating a figment of their imagination. I knew the truth. I was not valiant and I was without honor.

I reached into my backpack and pulled out the remnant container of pills. Taking no consideration for the ramifications, I went into the men's bathroom and swallowed as many as I had left. One pill, two pill, red pill, blue pill.

By now I was definitely feeling the aftermath of drinking on an empty stomach. I walked outside to the parking lot, avoiding any attention. With a violent heave, I hurled into the weeds beside Ryan's truck. My head was spinning, but I was feeling invincible. I put my backpack on over my shoulder and began the short walk down Fairview Road in the dark. Although I knew I was in bad shape, stumbling as I tried my best to navigate the dark roads, I figured I could make it to Sierra's house before passing out.

I walked with deliberate intention, two miles along the country road. In the distance I could see colors exploding in the sky. The skyrockets and fireworks were lighting up an otherwise cloudy night sky. Even the moon seemed to be hiding from me, or maybe I was hiding from the moon? It was Independence Day, and I was enslaved to the bondage of the past.

From a quarter of a mile away, I could see her light. Sierra always left it on, but I hoped she was still at the Bastians' house. I just wanted to crash on her couch and wake up with a headache and hope it was all just a bad dream.

But as I stumbled up the driveway, the front door opened and there she stood. She must have been watching for me, or perhaps she had a suspicion that this day was coming. I walked slowly toward her light, until she could see me clearly. Sierra stepped on to the front porch and stood motionless. She tilted her head to the side, suspiciously. And then just like she had done a thousand times before, she put her hands on her hips.

"Jordan," she said softly. "Where have you been?"

I had heard that question a thousand times, and every time I would give her an honest answer. "I've been up to no good, Sierra."

She stood there in the silhouette of the shining light, and I could see disappointment flickering in her eyes. It had been a long time since I'd stumbled down her driveway drunk and disorderly. We stood in silence until she could see the tears in my eyes.

I killed him.

Chapter 14

This Little Light Of Mine

Sierra stood frozen, confused. I trembled toward the steps, as the tears fell freely down my face. Although I was clearly under the influence of alcohol, reality jolted me back to momentary stone-cold sobriety. As I neared her, Sierra did not flinch. The door was still propped open behind her, and I could hear music playing softly inside.

I stopped at the bottom of the steps and fell to my knees. "It was me." All of a sudden, the words began to spill out of my mouth, and I couldn't keep silent any longer. Withholding the regret was as futile as trying to fend off an avalanche with a snow shovel. The words poured out, however disjointed and discombobulated, the confession was ripe. "I couldn't see clearly, and I panicked. We were all under attack, and swinging in the dark. I called for reinforcements, but when Cam came to the rescue, I pulled the trigger. Sierra, I couldn't tell anyone that the bullet came from my gun because I had been drinking, and I had drugs in my system. I fled the scene and hoped to God that nobody would ever find out."

After wiping my eyes, I looked up at her. She hadn't moved, but the words were still sinking in. I was getting lightheaded and thirsty, crying profusely. I crawled up the stairs toward her feet and begged, "Please, forgive me! I can't live like this. I am so sorry. I don't know what else to say." I reached toward her bare feet, and held on for dear life.

"*You...* shot Cam?" she whispered.

I nodded my head, but I couldn't show eye contact. I continued to lie at her feet, completely broken. She slowly repeated, "You pulled the trigger... and you never told anyone the truth about what happened to him?" The question seemed to hang in the air like breath leaving the lungs on a cold day. I nodded and admitted, "I was afraid."

My hopes in confessing this painful memory was to be set free from the torturous thoughts, and to live happily ever after, forgiven. But the aftermath of such a traumatic revelation would have immediate consequences.

Sierra stepped back from my reach, and exploded in righteous indignation. The cognitive wheels were spinning, and after she deliberated over the puzzle pieces, she realized I was the monster who had killed the love of her life. To her, I was the terrorist. "You are a liar! Everything about you is a lie. Your whole reality is based on a fictitious account with honorable medals for your acts of courage!"

She was just getting started.

"You have the audacity to high-five strangers and let them buy you drinks for being a war hero. You receive government paychecks each month for your valiant service and even have a 'Purple Heart' license plate that gets you out of speeding tickets! Worst of all, you're sharing a life with the widow and the daughter of the man you murdered, while you were hiding from the truth about your identity." She pointed back down the driveway, emphatically.

"Get out!"

She turned her back quickly and ran into the house. In the blink of an eye, she slammed the door and turned off the light. And all at once, the reality that I had fallen in love with seemed to be deconstructed by my confession. For the first time in my life, Sierra closed her door to me, and she would no longer "leave the light on."

I picked myself up from the ground and tried to make my way back to the road. But without the assistance of the porch light, I couldn't see. I was literally lost in the darkness, still spinning from the drunken confession and the implications of having burned the only bridge I ever needed. I stood in the driveway, unsure as to where to go or what to do.

This is exactly why I kept things hidden for so long. My greatest fear had become true. Jack Nicholson was right: People can't handle the truth of depravity. And when you're placed in a position of public trust, the expectation of constant integrity is not optional. So the decision to remain isolated in shame is founded on the exaggerated assumptions of the ripple effect. How will my confession help Sierra in any way? Will Karis grow up with abandonment issues because I'm not around anymore? Will she even remember me? What will happen when the people who believed and trusted me are devastated to learn I'm actually human?

Maybe I should have kept my mouth shut. Perhaps I should not have waivered on the investment that, although I wasn't a hero, I would never release the dastardly secrets of what really happened on that fateful day. Or maybe I was destined to be an addict, like my dad. It seemed that my own self-destructive choices would meet the inevitable end of life in prison or death by suicide.

Or maybe I was at a fork in the road of my life.

What if there was still time to find redemption? The healing path would be a challenging, narrow, uphill clawing that would demand wholeness and transparency. This road seemed to be the only way to rightly honor Cameron, and live in the overflow of gratitude.

As I stood in the driveway under the cover of darkness, I knew that I had two choices: I could become bitter, or I could become better. I did not want to end up like my father, alone and enslaved to his shame. I truly wanted to live in freedom, and to allow people to see the truth of my fractured integer in order for them to be able to fully love me.

Chapter 15

Twelve Steps Home

I wandered the streets for the most of the night, intoxicated with shame yet sobered by hope. Having been stranded without a vehicle or a working cell phone, I walked for hours back toward town. The silent majority of my thoughts were settled on a resolution to let go of the past and pursue my future. I refused to spend one more day letting my past mistakes determine my permanent identity.

I followed the winding roads under barren streetlights and a hidden moon. The clouds threatened like a growling dog with no bite. I walked in the midnight heat wishing the rolling thunder would unleash a torrential downpour.

It wasn't until I neared my apartment that I felt the first drops of rain. It couldn't have come at a better time, as I had begun to perspire through my shirt. For the last two miles, I marched on like a runner toward the finish line. The clouds dissipated, but the rain continued to fall like cosmic tears from a broken-hearted Father. I felt like a lost son coming home to a concerned papa, as he waited in the driveway with binoculars. I had once heard Pastor Ryan talking about the story of the prodigal son, and the lovesick father who ran to embrace him. He described the culture of the ancient world and how Aristotle once said, 'A proud man takes slow steps.' He concluded that the parable of Jesus described God as a father running without concern for propriety – *what does that tell us about the posture of heaven?* I could never resonate with the language of the Christian subculture that often referred to "Father God." My own dad was a violent and abusive drunk, and I used to imagine "Father God" as an angry terrorist who delighted in lightning bolts and genocide.

By the time I made it back to my apartment, the sun was beginning to illuminate the eastern sky. I quietly unlocked my apartment door so I wouldn't wake my mother, crept silently toward my bedroom, and collapsed like a fallen tree onto my mattress. I looked, smelled, and felt like a train had hit me, but I knew this was going to change everything.

Although my body was exhausted, my mind could not rest. I tossed and turned for a few hours before surrendering to the bathtub. I was too tired to stand up for a shower, so I crashed into the deep end of the tub and ran the water over my legs. Looking over my body, I saw the scabs and scars and dirt and grime and shame and beauty of a runaway slave. I began to scrub my skin clean, rinsing like a baptism of holy water.

My mother must have slipped out while I had been sleeping. She left a full pot of coffee on a timer for me, and as I got dressed I scribbled a note for her and left it on the counter.

Dear Mom,

Thank you for putting up with me all these years. I am so sorry for my selfishness, and for not treating you with more sensitivity. It's time for me to change, and I promise you, I am committed to the journey and will do whatever it takes to get there.

The manager of Whitey's Surf Shop gave me the contact information to the towing company that held my car. Aunt Tracy transported me in her God-forsaken station wagon, and lectured me the whole way. She was rambling on about choices and consequences and yada, yada, yada, but I just kept nodding. Yes, choices have consequences; I am well aware.

Once I was able to get my car released, I drove directly to see Pastor Ryan at church. The parking lot was empty, and the doors were locked. I assumed he'd be on vacation because of the holiday weekend, but I desperately wanted to get his guidance. While I was walking back to the parking lot, a vehicle pulled into the space next to mine. A tall Korean man nodded through his open window.

"Hey, there," he smiled, exiting his car. "Are you here for the meeting? You're a few minutes early, but I can let you in now."

I shook my head. "What meeting? I just wanted to talk to the pastor." The stranger with the kind eyes apologized. "Oh, I'm sorry. I assumed you were here for the Alcoholics Anonymous meeting. We meet in the church basement on Tuesday, Thursday, and Saturday afternoons."

I looked at my watch and asked, "What time does it start? I might be able to stick around for a bit." This was, of course, the orchestration of divine intervention. I was beginning to feel the mysterious presence of God at every corner. It was time to get help, and get honest about my brokenness.

Once inside, I helped make coffee and set up chairs. As more anonymous strangers joined the circle, I was warmly welcomed. Looking around the table, I saw a mosaic of beautiful pieces. Behind each name was a face and behind each face was a story. The diversity of outcasts and refugees presented an inexplicable acceptance of fellow pilgrims. I listened intently to the confessions of addicts "getting current," without hesitation. There was an assumed urgency to the conversations, and zero time for sugarcoated exaggerations. Three days of sobriety were as enthusiastically celebrated just as much as three years.

When it came to my turn to share, I was obviously granted the freedom to remain silent. But I was so inspired by the courageous transparency around the table that I couldn't hide behind a mask anymore. "Hello," I said. "My name is Jordan, and I'm an alcoholic and an addict." My voice was quivering, and my spine was selling out. Immediately I was met with the invasion of a communal reception, "Hi, Jordan."

I held both hands around my empty Styrofoam cup. "I don't know where to begin. My best friend always asks me where I've been, and I always say, 'I've been up to no good.' And the truth is, it's safe to be vague. But until now, I have never been specific or clear about where, exactly, I've been." I paused. The contemplation of how much detail to give was a matter of life and death. So I just opened my mouth and let the words fall out.

"I've been running and hiding from my past. My hands are shaking, and I'm guilty of self-destruction. I've been self-medicating with painkillers and booze for several years. I have been living a lie, being celebrated for something I'm not. I'm still healing from horrific memories of sirens and screams. I hate myself, but I don't want to live like this anymore."

I took a white chip, representing a commitment to sobriety: one day at a time. That meeting would be the first day of a new beginning. I walked away with the sudden relief of confession and the weightlessness of transparency. It felt so good to be in the company of other people with similar struggles. For the first time in my life, I felt the warm embrace of true acceptance, and the encouragement to return to the next meeting for another go around.

Everything changed. From the inside out, I was inhaling truth and exhaling shame. I went to Barnes & Noble to purchase a leather-bound journal, and began to record my thoughts and prayers. I read the scriptures with an exhaustive hunger, and I found a verse that said if I search for God with all of my heart, I would find him. So I closed my eyes and I prayed for God to show himself to me.

And every day, I found him. He was not very good at hiding… much like a little girl in the "wiving room" hiding under a blanket. God must love being found! I discovered Him in the laughter of children playing in the park. I tripped over God in the garden, among the sprouting petunias and the Black-Eyed Susans. I caught Him waving to me in the colors of the sunset, and smiling to me in the sunrise. I crashed into God in the most unlikely of places: conversations with my Dr. Bailey, in the mercy of a patrolman who was warning me about a speeding ticket. God was in the silence of the rising tide, and the ominous stillness of the midnight hour. I used to wonder where God was when I needed a miracle, but suddenly I was having a hard time finding any evidence of God's absence.

But most importantly, God was in my heart, all the time. He was growing like a wildfire in a hurricane blowing through my soul… I could not contain the transformation! I continued to attend every meeting I could, "getting current" and making new friends. The proclivity to chase away my anxiety with a pill or a bottle was revolutionized by contentment. I no longer felt anxious, and my dark nightmares faded.

I started meeting with Pastor Ryan on Saturday mornings for coffee. He began to speak into my life, words of healing and forgiveness. I never mentioned the details of Cameron's death, only that I had been living with a lot of condemnation and self-hatred. Pastor Ryan talked to me about the healing power of Jesus Christ and the invitation to accept his love. He taught me that all of my impulses to earn my own redemption would never be enough to cover my debt, but that the blood of Jesus finished the work and my only appropriate response is to believe the good news. "Have you come to the end of yourself, Jordan? When you hit rock bottom, and realize that there is nothing you can do to earn your salvation, that's when you are ready to experience was true freedom feels like. In that brokenness you cry out to the Lord, and say, "'Here I am!'" Pastor Ryan spread his arms out to demonstrate the reception of a divine hug. "You are forgiven, Jordan. You are loved, and there's nothing you can do about it."

After thirty days, I exchanged my white chip in to the recovery process. I had been sober for an entire month, and committed to keep working through the necessary steps of inner healing. Every week, I seemed to grow deeper in my understanding of God's love, and I sought out ways to serve others in the community.

On Wednesday mornings I volunteered at the local Rescue Mission, serving breakfast to the homeless in our community. I learned their names, and would linger to sit at their tables and talk with them for hours on end. Some of them appeared at our meetings, and I developed some deep friendships.

On Friday afternoons, I became an after-school mentor for troubled youth in our city. There was a time when I could have used a voice of instruction, and I saw myself in the eyes of many of these kids. Some of them did not have a father, or were already accumulating a criminal record before they reached high school. I began to teach reading and writing skills to inner-city kids, offering words of encouragement. I began to wonder how my life would have turned out differently if only I had a mentor.

On Sunday mornings, I would load up my car with some of these teens and take them to breakfast under the condition that they would join me for church after. We would sit in the back of the church together, and I would make the kids listen and behave and shut up. After church, we would all play basketball in the vacant parking lot across the street. One time, I got a rebound.

Days turned into weeks, and weeks turned into months. I did not hear from Sierra, and I completely released the heartache to God. Pastor Ryan said that Sierra had joined another church, and she was doing fine. I respected her wishes for me to stay away, assuming she would reach out to me if she wanted to stay in contact.

But I missed her terribly. I thought about her every single hour. I missed the way she used to insist on stopping for ice cream on the way *to* church. I missed the way she was always late, blaming her toenail polish for taking so long to dry. I missed the way she used to curl up next to me on the couch, backing into me because, of course. I missed the way she used to get blisters on her fingers playing the guitar, and the way she used to run through the sprinklers giggling like a little girl. I missed the way she used to demand her marshmallows to be burnt to a crisp; otherwise, they were considered raw and inedible. I missed the way she used to try to spell my name in her alphabet soup, and play footsies with me under the table. I missed the way she used to listen to her playlists for inspiration when working out, and how her favorite song was the Rocky theme. She would do sit-ups in the living room, and pretend she was boxing Ivan Drago. I missed the way she would lift her hands when singing in church, and closed her eyes to pray.

And I missed Karis. It is without wonder that her name means "grace." Her relentless pursuit of my heart taught me that I was unconditionally accepted. I missed that little girl so much! I missed the way she used to untie my shoes, only to practice tying them again. I missed the way she used to practice cartwheels on the church lawn, looking around to see if anyone was watching. I missed the way she used to sing, "This little light of mine, I'm gonna let it shine…" I missed the way she used to emulate her mommy, painting her toenails a sloppy shade of everywhere. I missed the way she used to laugh until she farted, and then tried to blame it on me. I missed the creative endeavors she used to procrastinate at bedtime, not the least of which was a crisis or injury of some sort. I missed the way she carried Band-Aids in her pockets at all times, and an assortment of crayons. I missed the way she used to laugh and cry at the same time, and the way she never finished her meals, and the way she used to insist that I tell her a story about Timmy the Turtle and sing her exactly four songs every night before bedtime.

As the summer turned to fall, absence made the heart grow fonder. Not all is fair in love and war, because I lived in the paradox of profound sadness and unexplainable joy. I focused all of my energy on inner healing and spiritual recovery, choosing to love myself well so that I can truly love my neighbor. I became a more attentive son, seeking after the wellbeing of my mother. I picked up extra shifts at the lumber yard, and eventually got a raise. With the increased income, I was able to take my mom to her chiropractic appointments, and sometimes in the evening I would massage her shoulders, and she began to tell me stories about my dad.

My heart softened toward my father, and I realized that I had been carrying a deep resentment for many years. In one of my many coffee conversations with Pastor Ryan, he noticed that I rarely mentioned him.

"Have you forgiven your dad, Jordan?" he asked. I brushed off the question, and changed the subject. But in the following months, as my mother shared stories with me about his tenderness toward me in my toddler years, I was reminded of Pastor Ryan's inquiry. Forgiveness was such a complicated and multilayered topic, because I desperately wanted to be forgiven by Sierra, but I seemed to have given myself permission to hold my father hostage in my memory. Pastor Ryan once quoted Nelson Mandela, the legendary freedom fighter who had been wrongfully imprisoned during the South Africa Apartheid. He said, "Resentment is like drinking poison and then hoping it will kill your enemies." In other words, the bitterness that had built up inside me over the years had begun to eat away at my heart like cancer, and it was time to let it go.

So with the encouragement of Pastor Ryan and my mom, I took a road trip to the South Carolina State Penitentiary where my father had been living since I was twelve years old. I arrived early and waited anxiously with a growing number of other visitors who were all waiting to see their loved ones. A buzzer sounded, and a door opened.

My eyes searched for my father, as a line of inmates walked toward the open room, full of tables and chairs. I watched small children running to embrace their fathers, and hardened felons wiping away tears as they kissed their wives.

Toward the end of the line was a sad, old man with the eyes of my father, though if it had not been for his wave, I might not have known it was him. The years had not been kind to him, and he seemed to walk with a visible limp. He stood in front of me and extended his hand. "Hello, son." I took a step closer and bypassed his handshake, opting for a hug instead. He received my hug, and I felt his feeble shoulders trembling as I held him. "It's good to see you, Dad," I said softly.

We were only allowed forty-five minutes to catch up on over fifteen years of estrangement. As I told him about Baghdad, and Sierra, and Mom, and all of the things I had always wanted to tell him, he began to wipe away runaway tears. It seemed like regret had swallowed him alive, and now he was tasting forgiveness for the first time. The gray hairs were fading, and his once-strong arms were now weak. But he was my dad, and I chose to love him.

From that day forward, I vowed to write to him. And I would return each month, if only for an hour. There were years to catch up on, and we were haunted with the inevitable hope for an early release.

Thanksgiving came and went without hearing from Sierra. I secretly hoped I would have received an invitation to a feast to the unbroken circle in the some glad morning. But silence prevailed, and I grieved the death of what once was. My mother cooked a turkey, and we invited a few of the homeless veterans to our meal.

Although my heart still ached for Sierra and Karis, I was truly grateful to have the company of new friends.

I had managed to cobble together a good life. Although I continued to work out my salvation with fear and trembling, I gave thanks for the lessons learned along the way. Nothing would ever be the same from the way it was before, but then again, what once was wasn't authentic or honest, and I chose to walk a new path of wholeness. My continued counseling sessions with Dr. Bailey helped me to understand what it meant to have "integrity without being fractured."

I'm Gonna Let It Shine

Christmas morning did not provide the snow that we had hoped for, but it was blistery cold nonetheless. I refused to spend one more holiday without reaching out to the woman who saved my life. I loaded my car up with gifts, delicately wrapped (thanks, Mom!), with kisses and hugs for the two girls who meant more to me than anything in the world.

I took the back roads to the south side of town, driving past The Alibi and turning left on Fairview Road. From a distance, I could see the old farmhouse, and even the December frost couldn't keep the grass from shining emerald green. I saw the porch where we used to sit, swinging for hours. I brushed the tears aside as I slowly turned into the driveway.

After I turned off the ignition, I waited to see if the door would open or remain closed. In the window, I could the rosy cheeks of a little girl scurrying to see who was here. I opened my door and loaded up my arms with gifts, walking up the driveway...

It felt like home.

I stood trembling in the presence of grace as Sierra emerged from the front door. Despite the cold December wind, she refused to put on a jacket or shoes. Her hair was longer since the last time I'd seen her, and she maintained the atomic beauty that held me captive all these years.

Somewhere between then and now, I must have become unrecognizable to her. Where shame had painted my conscience with self-inflicted scars, mercy covered the wounds. I was no longer afraid to look in her eyes, and in this moment I could not turn away.

Sierra stood like a silhouette on the front porch. She locked eyes with me as she put both hands on her hips.

"Jordan," she said quietly.

"Where have you been?"

In that moment, Karis came bolting out the front door and down the steps. She was six years old now, and knew enough to understand the significance of the moment. I dropped the load of gifts as she jumped into my arms, kissing me and hugging me and laughing. She just kept interrupting her questions with kisses and squealing, while I just held her tightly in my arms. She whispered in my ear, "I told Santa that I wished for you to come back!"

Clutching Karis tightly, I carried her up the steps to face Sierra. Standing face to face, I spoke with confident humility and holistic honesty. For the first time in my life, I could answer this question with gratitude.

"Where have I been?" I repeated her question. "Thanks for asking... I've been working out my salvation with fear and trembling. I've been going to church. I've been volunteering at the Rescue Mission. I've been mentoring troubled teens. I've been attending recovery meetings and getting counseling. I've been searching for God, and finding Him in every corner of my life." I set Karis down briefly to kneel down on one knee before Sierra.

"And I've come here to tell you that I love you, and I always will. I am homeless unless you are with me, and I want to spend the rest of my life pursuing your heart. The past is erased as far as the east is from the west, but the remaining chapters of our lives are still being written." I pulled out a small jewelry box from my front pocket and opened it up to reveal a diamond ring. "I will never stop asking for your heart and your hand in marriage. Will you give me the honor of spending the rest of my life loving you?"

Sierra did not move, except to brush away a runaway tear. In her impatience, Karis walked up to her mommy and kicked her in the shins. "Say yes, Mommy!"

Sierra smiled at me, taking two steps backwards.

She continued to not say a word, then opened the door and turned on the light.

Epilogue

S even months later, I sat with Karis beside the beach. She was wearing a pink swimsuit, covered in sand and sunblock, a tiny, plastic shovel in her left hand. She pointed at me and commanded, "You can use the bucket to help me!" And together we began the construction of an epic castle in the sand.

Sierra was half asleep in the summer sun, listening to the waves rolling in softly near her bare feet. She was drenched in beauty, exploding in the violent fragility of all things reverent. It was the Fourth of July, exactly one year from the traumatic confession that changed our lives forever. I began to think about Cameron, and I wondered if it was time to tell Karis stories about her father.

"Did you know that your daddy and I used to surf over there?" I said, pointing to the beach break in the near distance. She paused and looked over to the scope of my finger and squinted, as if to look for any remains of her father's legacy.

While I continued to talk, I worked tenaciously at the construction of a security wall around the sand castle. And of course, every sand castle needs a moat filled with crocodiles!

"And over there," I said, and pointed up the beach to a pavilion under a trio of palm trees, "is where your mommy and daddy got married!" Once again, Karis looked in immaculate wonder toward the memory that she would only read or hear about. I looked at her adorable dimples and said, "Karis, you have your daddy's eyes. You know, he would be so proud of you."

She tilter her head briefly, looking at me with a toothless grin. We resumed to the blue prints of architectural genius. After a few minutes of evaluation, Karis watched me putting the last finishing touches on the wall around the castle.

"What are you doing?" She yelled at me, as if I had ruined her whole existence. I explained that to her that every castle needs to have a gate around it to keep the bad guys out. She stood up and put her hands on her hips, just like her mommy. "Not my castle. I want a big front door!" Karis smashed the wall with a feminine fist, and carved out an exaggerated entrance to her castle of grace.

Grace.

Scandalous grace. Mysterious grace. Amazing grace. Bang-my-head–against-the wall grace. Knock-me-off-my-feet grace. Incomprehensible grace. Violent grace. Furious grace. Bloody grace. Terrible grace. Awful grace. Inexplicable grace. Stand–up-and-sing grace. Sit–down-and cry grace. Gospel grace. New World Disorder grace. Upside-down grace. Inside-out grace. Crucified grace. Resurrected grace. The last chapter is still being written about grace. Redeeming grace. Prostitute-turned-princess grace. Body-broken, blood-poured-out grace. Welcome to the table of grace. Pull-up-a-chair grace. Light–a-candle-grace. Beautiful fingerprints of grace.

Printed in the United States
By Bookmasters